CLOSE TO DEATH

THE SENSITIVES BOOK THREE

RICK WOOD

BLOOD SPLATTER PRESS

RICK WOOD

Rick Wood is a British writer born in Cheltenham.

His love for writing came at an early age, as did his battle with mental health. After defeating his demons, he grew up and became a stand-up comedian, then a drama and English teacher, before giving it all up to become a full-time author.

He now lives in Loughborough, where he divides his time between watching horror, reading horror, and writing horror.

ALSO BY RICK WOOD

The Sensitives
The Sensitives
My Exorcism Killed Me
Close to Death
Demon's Daughter
Questions for the Devil
Repent
The Resurgence
Until the End

The Rogue Exorcist
The Haunting of Evie Meyers
The Torment of Billy Tate
The Corruption of Carly Michaels

Chronicles of the Infected
Zombie Attack
Zombie Defence
Zombie World

Non-Fiction
How to Write an Awesome Novel
Horror, Demons and Philosophy

THEN

Edinburgh, Scotland
2008

1

As Derek's placed his tense foot into the sparse gaps of empty floor, his thoughts could barely process what he was witnessing.

It was a slaughter. Practically genocide. So many children, so many young lives lost. Some of them would have only just learnt to talk. Just learnt to read. To write.

Now their remains were only vaguely recognisable as features of mutilated bodies.

As his feet absentmindedly carried him through the various rooms of the house, it was all the same. Fresh blood trickling down ripped wallpaper. Limbs left askew across various ornaments. Bodies left inside out.

And their faces. Their wretched, wide eyes. Their innocent pale skin. Their mouths twisted to a frown or contorted to a scream.

Deadly still.

Never to move again. Never to breathe a flicker of hair out of their faces. Never to tell an adoptive parent they loved them. Never to be given the luxury of growing old.

This couldn't have been her. It couldn't have been.

Just as the thought hit him, he saw a flutter of a dress outside the window. Beyond the trees, beyond the twisting path, directed to the edge of the nearby hill.

Was that her?

"So," came the furious Scottish accent of a police officer appearing in the doorway. "You still telling me that this was the wee work of a demon?"

Derek said nothing. He knew there were no words he could give that would appease the tragic, unspeakable events that had occurred in this formerly warm abode.

So he just stared. Looked into the eyes of the furious man glaring back into his.

"Pathetic. You come here with your religious nonsense, telling us we can rely on you. That we need to be patient."

"Which you weren't," Derek spoke, against his better judgement. "You weren't patient. And you didn't rely on me. That's why this has happened."

"*Get out!*" screamed the officer, his skin a shade of red similar to that of the splattered walls.

It was not a good decision to stay. Derek had seen what he needed to see and said what he wished to say. Without meeting the man's eyes, he stepped lightly down the stairs and out of the house.

He pursued the path, leaving the chaos of the crime scene behind him. He followed it between the twisting trees until he came to an opening. The opening was beside a steep hillside, which he followed. The vertical drop below his feet made his legs quiver, but he had to rely on his resolve.

Because this is where he found her.

Alone. Torn. Unable to cope.

Close up, he could see the destruction on her face. A formerly happy-go-lucky, spritely nineteen-year-old girl now stood solemnly, with the crust of dried blood weighing down her filthy dress and her mouth bathed in red that still trickled from her lips.

"Madelina," Derek spoke, softly and reassuringly. He did his best to show by his voice that he was not judging her, that he was not blaming her. He knew that, whilst her hands were covered in guilt, it was not her mind that had commanded them to commit the actions she had committed. "Please. Don't move."

Her head slowly twisted toward him. Her cheeks were stained with tears. Her hair was contorted into a scraggly mess. Bags sat so prominently under her bloodshot eyes it looked like a permanent shadow. She stood feebly, her knees trembling, on the edge of the sharp drop.

She was a wreck, no doubt about it. And Derek could completely understand why.

"Madelina, please. Don't."

"Don't?" she whispered back at him. "Did you see what I did?"

Her acknowledgement of what had occurred forced more tears to her eyes. They erupted down her face, dripping onto her collar, her body convulsing in mortified guilt.

"But you didn't do it," Derek said. "Did you?"

"Look at me."

"Yes, but–"

"*Look at me!*" her whisper turned to a scream, her voice breaking under the strain of her shout.

Derek glanced over his shoulder, hoping that no one had heard.

"I am. I am looking at you."

"Does it not look like I did this?" she asserted. "Does it not look like it was by my hands? By my… my teeth."

Her head dropped. Her eyelids pushed together. She could not look at him any longer.

"Madelina, listen to me–"

"I ate them, Derek," she continued, her voice quivering, convulsing, returning to a low whisper that almost got carried away on the breeze. "I ripped them apart. They are in me. Right now, I can feel them, turning in my stomach. I can feel my body digesting them."

"It wasn't you, Madelina."

"Look at me–"

"I *am* looking at you, Madelina. But we've talked about this. It's what's inside you. It's what's controlling you."

"What's controlling me?"

"She is. Lamia. You know this, I've told you this. Please, let me help you, I can get rid of it."

"And what if you do? Huh? What if you do?"

Derek's voice faltered.

"They are hardly going to forgive me, are they? The evidence won't work in court. I'll be in the press as – as the girl who ate… *babies…* and claimed she was possessed. How would that look?"

"You have to believe in people, Madelina. It's the only way."

Madelina shook her head with such adamant refusal that Derek began to feel her slip away. She was out of arm's reach, and he knew that if he edged toward her, it would only make things worse. He was relying entirely on his words, in hope that he could string a sentence together that would convince her against what she so stubbornly believed was the truth.

"People are good. You are good. You *have* to believe that. Or… or then, well – then you are lost."

"I wish I could believe in people the way you do, Derek."

Her eyes turned toward the heavy drop. She was inches away. Just inches.

"All you need to do is see it. It's there. You just need to look at people, and–"

Derek did not have time to finish his sentence.

She threw herself with all the force she could, and she fell hard, into the abyss of the sudden, deep drop.

By the time Derek reached the hillside, retracted the arms he'd flung toward her and peered below, she was already dead.

Her upturned body and broken neck were just visible in the small lines that surrounded her body.

2

MARTIN'S FEET COULD BARELY FIND A SPACE VOID OF BLOOD OR mayhem.

He had barely made his way through the open doorway before he toppled back, collapsed on the front porch and vomited his morning's healthy portion of Weetabix over the welcome mat.

He couldn't turn his head back. But he knew that he must. He had to see it. If there was any way he could have gotten away without seeing it, he would have. If there was some way he could have let his legs carry him away through the fields, away from the house, full of blissful ignorance, he would have done.

But this was his and Derek's doing. This girl was their responsibility. And she had – no, that *thing* inside of her womb had – ripped apart a building full of vulnerable, helpless, young children.

His eyes traced the floor, his head lolling as he forced it to rotate just a little more, until finally, the inside of the house came into his vision.

Dear God.

Eaten. So many of them, eaten. But only partially. Why?

Why only partially?

Were they still alive when she did this?

He couldn't. He couldn't look. It was not something he could bear to comprehend.

Not yet.

Not ever.

He pushed himself to his feet and staggered to the driveway as he attempted to walk away, unable to keep his balance. After falling onto his open palms, he brushed the gravel onto his jeans and traipsed back to the car. He used it for support as he collapsed upon it, burying his face in his arms.

He had told Derek.

Dammit, why had he told Derek?

Because Derek normally knows best.

Normally.

But, no. Not this time. Derek had insisted. This heavily pregnant woman was too weak for an exorcism. She wouldn't survive it. They had to wait until the child was born and hope for the best.

"Believe in hope," Derek had told Martin, his ever-wise words endowing their worldly knowledge upon him. "Believe in good. It's what we pray to when we exorcise a demon, but we don't always need an exorcism for it to help us."

That was Derek's solution to everything.

A positive outlook.

Martin had served by his side during The Edward King War. He had learnt so much from him. He had been plucked out of his youth at just fifteen years old and coerced into a battle that was far bigger than he was.

Why? Because heaven had conceived him. As a backup plan. As the solution to their mess of trusting hell. Of hoping for the best.

He was the first Sensitive.

He was heaven's solution for hoping for the best.

But he hadn't been Derek's.

Derek, who had taught him everything he knew.

Derek, who had not only let Martin down, but Madelina, and the entire orphanage that lay in shreds behind him.

From a distance, Derek's figure approached, cast in a smooth silhouette from the evening sun. As he grew closer, Martin could see that his head was down and he was in a deep, contemplative trance.

Martin didn't care.

"You!" he spat, as soon as Derek came close enough to hear.

Derek waved away the hostility, unwilling to engage.

"Don't wave me away!" Martin growled. "Have you seen what she has done?"

Derek paused by the car. Not looking at Martin. Not looking anywhere but down. A fallen face. A body bereft, void of energy.

"Don't ignore me," Martin insisted. "Have you seen–"

"Yes!" Derek interrupted with a hasty annoyance. "Yes, I have bloody well seen what she has done."

"And? And what are you–"

"She's dead."

Martin's words fell short.

He didn't know what to think. Anger at Derek? Sadness at her death? Relief that her suffering was over?

"How?" Martin demanded.

"She wouldn't listen to reason, she – she threw herself off."

"And what do you have to say about that?"

Derek frowned.

"What the hell do you mean, what do I have to say about that?"

"Because I told you! *I* told *you*! She needed an exorcism, she needed–"

"She was eight months bloody gone, Martin."

"So?"

"We needed to trust in hope."

"Yeah? You seen what hope has done? Have you?" Martin's fists clenched, his whole body tensed, lurching forward, ready to unleash. "Go have a look why don't you?"

"I have."

"And have you seen the guts? The blood? The pieces of children?"

"Go to hell, Martin."

Derek opened the car door.

"No, Derek, you can't–"

"Martin, stop."

Martin watched Derek. He could see Derek's pain. Could see the look on his face. Could see how much this mistake was eating him up inside, in a way that Derek probably hadn't completely come to terms with yet.

How could you?

How could you ever come to terms with–

Martin's head dropped.

He had said it. Insisted they should exorcise her, pregnant or not, that she could take it. Derek hadn't listened to him. This could have been avoided, if only Derek had listened to him. If he had *listened.* But he hadn't. He hadn't listened, and now–

"No," Martin decided. "Tell you what, Derek. *You* go to hell."

Martin turned and walked away.

That was the last time they ever saw each other alive.

Worcester, England
2014

3

A CONDUIT.

When April had first been introduced to the word, she had looked it up in the dictionary. It told her that she was either:

1. *A channel for conveying water or other fluid.*
2. *A tube or trough for protecting electric wiring.*

Being fairly sure that she was neither a water carrier nor an electrical conductor, she had decided that she would have to relearn everything she knew.

A drastic conclusion to come to, but one that undoubtedly proved true throughout the subsequent years.

"Right, so, erm – what?" April asked.

"A conduit," Julian repeated for the nth time that hour. "That is what you are. A conduit."

"I thought I was a Sensitive?"

"Yes, you are, but different Sensitives have different gifts. All right? I am good at exorcisms and detecting other Sensitives. You are a–"

"Yeah, a conduit, I get that." She nodded, her youthful

exuberance beginning to wear down Julian's patience. "But what is a conduit? I mean, what do I do?"

"A conduit acts as a host for whatever spirit, demon, or undead we are trying to contact."

"A host? What, like, for a party?"

Julian rubbed his sinus. Took a few breaths. Lifted his head again.

"No," he answered with clear pronunciation. "You are a host, as in, you let them use your body."

"I let a dead person use my body?" April repeated, her face scrunched into repulsion. "That's icky! I don't want a dead dude in me!"

"Technically, it's the undead spirit. It allows us to speak to them."

"And what do I do while you are speaking to them, and all that?"

"You feel them."

April's repulsed face grew more extreme.

"I don't mean like that!" Julian said with exasperation. "As in, whilst you are host to their spirit, you will be able to feel that dead person's feelings. Maybe even see their memories. They will show you who they are."

"I still don't get how I'm supposed to do that."

Julian allowed an irritated smile to spread itself across his reddening cheeks.

"Do you trust me?" he asked.

"What?"

"I said, do you trust me?"

"Well, yeah, I guess."

"Then you will allow me to show you."

Julian lit the three candles placed carefully around April. He turned off the lights, meaning the living room was lit by nothing but a flickering amber glow.

"We came to this house because of a spirit that won't leave

it. I need you to see what its memories are. See what happened. Why it's still here."

"How do I do that?"

"You close your eyes and concentrate. Erase all thought. Go blank as I recite my prayer."

April huffed.

"Fine."

She closed her eyes. Wiped her thoughts. Concentrated.

Thought about that turkey sandwich waiting for her in the fridge back home.

No! No thoughts!

She compelled the turkey sandwich from her mind and focused on her breathing.

Nothing but her breathing.

In. Out. Deep breaths.

Her mind grew blissfully clear.

Calm.

Tranquil.

In. Out.

Deep breaths.

"The spirit of the Lord be with me," Julian's voice spoke clearly and articulately. "He hath anointed me to preach to the unwilling, to those that remain. In the name of the Lord, as we pray that he will forgive our sins, we pray that he reveals yours."

She felt her mind slip into a steady absence.

She was there. Aware. But in the way that you can see through the windscreen of a car from the backseat.

Her arms became loose. Her legs grew hollow. Her mind faded to blank.

"To the Saviour, show us the unclean spirit. Allow them to reveal themselves, so we can help them move on."

Deeper and deeper into the trance.

Sinking further.

"Spirit in this room, I call on you now. Use this vessel to show us your past, and show us your purpose."

A flicker of thought pounced itself like the fire in a lighter, then evaporated just as clearly.

April could see it in her mind, as clear as her own thoughts.

But they weren't her thoughts.

They didn't feel anything like her thoughts.

"Show us."

A living room.

The living room she was in, but older. The furniture was different. More... retro. Flowery. Furniture like a grandparent would have.

Her hands were wrinkly. Old. Veins stuck out like exposed wiring in a faulty cable.

Before her was a little girl.

Anger.

She felt anger. A little sadness, but mostly anger.

"I don't feel like speaking," she said, but not in her voice. It was old and croaky, like that of an old man. She could feel her mouth moving, but her voice remained dormant.

That child. That girl. Beneath her greying hands.

The girl screamed.

"This is my home," the old man's voice exclaimed through her unwilling lips.

Those hands. They wrapped themselves around the child's throat.

Hostility.

They squeezed.

Rage.

They tightened until her breath pushed itself out of her throat and she could breathe no more.

"My home!"

Fury.

Scorn.

Wrath.

Every form of anger flowed through her, like a painful ache after running too fast. They pulled on her muscles like weights, filled her thoughts with rabid desire to kill, to hate, to maim this child, to rip her apart.

She looked down.

The child's body was limp.

"My home!"

Her body convulsed upwards, stiffening into a plank, held rigidly for a few moments.

She heard Julian uttering a few desperate prayers, holding a cross against her chest. She was held there until his prayers finished and her body could fall limp again, at which point she flopped like a discarded puppet on the ground.

Julian rushed to her side.

"We heard his voice," he told her. "He spoke through you. Did you hear it?"

She nodded frenziedly, her thoughts trying to make sense of what she had seen.

"I saw…"

"What? What did you see?"

"I saw…"

"What, April, what?"

She closed her eyes. Willed her panting to stop. Gathered her rambles into coherent thoughts that made sense.

Everything changed in that moment.

Her knowledge. Her worldview. Her purpose.

Everything became new.

"I saw him. I saw him strangle a child. A girl."

"Good, April. You saw what he had done."

She cried. Tears poured. She covered her face, not wanting to seem weak, but unable to control the frantic despair that she had been made to feel.

"What is it, April? What is it?"

17

"I felt anger… I wanted to kill her… I wanted to…"

"*You* didn't want to, April. *He* did."

It made sense. Those final few words from Julian made it all fit in place.

She was a conduit.

She felt the feelings of the dead. Of others.

She hated it. It had hurt her, scarred her mind with feelings she would never be able to forget.

Yet she had a feeling it was only the first of many.

NOW

Gloucester, England
2018

(8 MONTHS)

4

THE DUVET COCOONED TOMMY IN A SHIELD OF SILENCE, TRAPPED alone with the smell of sweat and sickness.

His arms shook – out of fear or illness, he could not tell. Possibly both. The small amount of blood left in his body raced through his hollow veins. Tears formed in the corner of his eyes, causing a half-moon crescent blur across his vision, masking the darkness he had encompassed himself within.

He closed his eyes. Tight. As much as he could. As if it would change anything. As if closing his eyes and refusing to listen would mean that nothing was there.

For a moment, his erratic breathing was the only thing disturbing the slumber throughout the children's ward of the hospital, and he wished he was at home. He wished he had his mummy's arms to envelop him in safety. He had begged her not to go, pleaded for her to stay after visiting times were over, but she had to be wrenched away by the nurses, insisting it was time for the children on the ward to sleep, insisting she would just have to come back in the morning.

Insisting that Tommy had to face this night alone.

Another night. Another absent sleep. Another terrified

darkness, counting down the minutes, the hours, until the curtains would be opened and sunlight would bathe him in relief once more.

For it was only at night it came. Only night.

The night was still in its infancy, almost as young as his eight-year-old self, yet to grow into the full, ferocious force that the night's adolescence would bring.

At school they had told him to pray to God. When he was scared, afraid, or worried, to put his hands together and pray. That vicar that came to visit him, who made him laugh, he tried to help him believe in such a notion.

But prayer did nothing for those other boys. Prayer did nothing for that girl who died of her cancer two days ago. The girl he used to play with, laugh with, until he awoke one morning to find an empty bed.

Prayer did nothing for the boy who woke with a large scar down his chest. The police officer told them not to be worried, that nothing was going to get them, that this was a one-off.

But there was still that look in his eye. That look where his lips spoke of reassurance, but his eyes spoke of confusion. How something could sneak in and tear a child apart in the middle of a children's ward without being noticed was beyond him.

It was beyond any of them.

Tommy looked at his watch. Pressed the light button and illuminated the Purple Power Ranger behind the clock hands.

It had been minutes. A few minutes down of so many.

He held his breath.

There it was.

That sound of a trickling, greasy tail sliding along solid floor. Like the squelch a wet slap against the side of a swimming pool, continuous in its hasty yet silent movement.

Tommy was tempted to look. Tempted to pull down the duvet to see what the monster looked like, to get an impression of what it was that tormented the ward every single mortifying night.

But he daren't.

If he looked at it, it would be real.

He kept his arms wrapped over his head, padding at the outside of his skull where his hair once was.

"Tommy…"

His eyes sprung open to the sound of his name, so subtle it could be mistaken for a breeze.

"Tommy…"

One could be forgiven for attributing the sound to other things. To the breathing of another child, the rustle of the bedsheets, the sudden gulp in his breath. But Tommy knew what he'd heard.

He knew.

It was a woman's voice. A sultry voice. It almost sounded human.

"Tommy… where are you…"

He shook his head. Put his hands over his eyes and furiously shook. The hairs on his arms stood on end, his spine turned to ice, but he refused.

No.

No, it can't be.

A faint shadow fell over the side of his duvet. He could see something.

A figure, but not. A face with too many features to be real. Fingers, but elongated into piercing claws. Large, exposed breasts contorted into skewwhiff directions. And a long, thick serpent tail flailing behind it.

"Tommy… I know you're there…"

"Go away!" he tried to shout, but it just came out as a croak. His voice had gone, disappeared with his courage.

How does no one else see it?

Why is it the nurses, the doctors, the parents, the visitors, the vicars, the patients, why – why is it only him and the really, really sick ever heard its crooked joints as they moved closer, breaking the stiffness of its bones with every flex?

They never heard its laughter, left under its breath, so quiet yet pounding against the inside of his skull.

They never heard its speaking. Its slow utterances, quivering with the fever of its joyous loathing.

The shadow stopped. Halted. Tommy buried his head in his lap, covered his ears, covered his eyes.

Just a few more hours till morning.

Just a few more hours till morning.

Just a few more hours till morning.

"I can... hear you... breathing..."

"Go away!"

"It's... your... turn..."

"Leave me alone!"

The duvet slid slowly along his skin. Lifting his head slightly, he saw the shadow of its claw twisting it away, pulling it off.

Tommy's hands reached out and clamped onto the duvet.

It did nothing.

It still slithered away, slithered like a wet snake, slipping between his fingers. He reached for it, grabbed it, did everything he could not to let it go.

It still did nothing.

The duvet was swept straight off.

He didn't look. He didn't let himself. He covered his face once more, burying his head between his legs, his hands over his ears, his eyes shut tight. Refusing. Refusing to let this thing into his life, to let it live, to let it get him. Refusing to be party to its games. Refusing to...

He shivered. He was cold. It was as if a frost had suddenly thrown itself like an icy cloth over his body. He had never felt so cold before.

His hands seized in convulsions of terror.

"Leave me alone…"

"Tommy… you know I can't…"

"No!"

Tommy screamed. A high-pitched, deafening, ear-piercing, shrill scream.

And just as he did that, he finally allowed his head to look up and stare into the eyes of his murderer.

The nurses did not find his corpse until morning.

5

APRIL'S PRIMARK PANTIES SLIPPED DOWN AROUND HER ANKLES, squeezed open by the pressure of the widening space between her Converses. She thrust the least expensive pregnancy test she had found in the pharmacy between her legs, and peered at the ceiling as she tried not to splash any urine on her hands.

Once she'd finished, she held the stick out in one hand, and her watch in the other.

A tuneless hum escaped her lips, quiet enough so as not to escape the sanctity of her cubicle. Anything to pass the long two minutes she had to wait, with partially sprinkled fingers, just to witness whether one line would turn into two.

The bustle of the toilet door opened and closed, and the high-heeled shoes of two girls with upper-middle-class accents entered, obviously put on – let's be fair, they were in the bathroom of a Wetherspoons – chatting about some girl who had put weight on.

My God. Am I going to put weight on?
No.
Stop it.

It hasn't even come back positive yet.

She glanced at her watch. Ninety-six seconds and counting.

"She totally, like, ballooned, and I was totally grossed out. I mean, like, a whale would have been thinner than her," came the uppity voice, with an upper inflexion rising at the end of the sentence as if her statement were a question.

Please, just sod off...

Seventy-two seconds.

"I totally cannot believe Dave ploughed her."

Ploughed?

Oh, wow. Jeeze. Classy bitches then.

April looked over the cubicle wall, scanning the graffiti with her dormant eyes. Apparently, Alison hearts Simon 4eva. Good for her.

There was also a random girl's phone number, the declaration that Jade is a slut, and the following quote: 'War doesn't say who is right, only who is left.'

That's just what I want in the middle of a pregnancy scare – ethics on war.

Her mind escaped the graffiti and turned to Oscar. Such a lovely young man, a perfect boyfriend. Geeky, yes. A little dweeby, absolutely – but a heart of gold. He adored April – probably because she was the first woman who ever looked at him for longer than three seconds without saying, "Excuse me, but why are you staring?"

April decided she was being cynical. Probably just pregnancy hormones.

Stop it! I don't know if I'm pregnant yet!

Fifty-four seconds.

Even though their relationship was still in its infancy, Oscar had been a devoted, faithful, loving boyfriend. He'd said the words *I love you* far before April had expected, and she'd taken him to bed probably far quicker than he expected, but they worked. They read each other's minds, finished each other's sentences, and could not bear spending a moment away from each other.

But he was still young. As was she.

Were they really ready to be parents?

How would he even react?

He'd probably go running for the hills.

No.

That's not true.

Not Oscar. He was a kind soul. He would never do anything to hurt her, and she knew it.

"Like, oh my God, Suzie, why are you wearing that shade? It totally clashes with my top."

Oh, dear God. Do people like this actually exist?

She pulled off some toilet paper and dabbed at her hands. The urine sprinkles as she'd held the test in place had gone. She lifted her fingers curiously to her nose, pulling back with repulsion at the smell.

Great. Dried piss stuck to fingers. *Just what I wanted.*

She scanned the other wall.

Apparently, Alison had also hearted Jack, Keith, and Andrew, but each of their names had been scribbled out.

How often does Alison use this cubicle anyway?

She checked her phone.

Thirty-six seconds.

She let out a large sigh, prompting her lips to vibrate in a long raspberry. This was the longest two minutes of her life. How could two minutes last so long?

Thirty-two seconds.

Uuuuurrrrrrgggggghhhhhh.

"Like, Suzie, you are totally splashing me with your water. Like, what the heck? Could you watch it?"

April felt sorry for Suzie.

She wondered what the faceless voices looked like. Suzie was probably incredibly normal, and her friend probably wore so much makeup she had a face like plaster. Maybe she worked in the makeup aisle in Boots, had a really bad fake tan, and wore every product she sold on her crusty, fading skin.

Twenty seconds.

Oh God.

No.

I'm not ready for the answer.

Got to chill out.

Fifteen seconds.

"Oh my God, Alison just texted me; the beast is coming out. Suzie, you totally cannot speak to her. I forbid it."

Jeeze, Suzie, grow a pair.

Ten seconds.

She began hyperventilating. She pushed the stick away from her, turning her head away, pushing the truth as far away from her eyes as she could.

Five seconds.

Tick-tock.

"Suzie, my life is, like, falling apart right now."

Three.

Two.

One.

April looked at the stick.

With a scream, she burst out of the cubicle and vomited over the sink, splashing Suzie's Armani makeup bag in the process.

She pulled her jeans up from around her ankles, fastened them, then threw up another mouthful of Weetabix.

"Oh my God, like, what are you doing?"

"Piss off, Suzie."

April looked at herself in the mirror. Her static hair waving in obscure directions, her skin pale, and her lip quivering beneath a splatter of sick.

In her mind, she could only think the same two words over, and over, and over again:

I'm pregnant.

(7 MONTHS)

6

THE COLD, STERILE WALLS OF THE HOSPITAL CORRIDOR CAUSED A rejected feeling of morbidity to settle in Julian's gut. What is it about these solid floors reflecting the long strips of white light, plain, pale walls vacant of decoration, and constant consecutive perfectly aligned rooms – what is it about them that always makes a person feel a tinge of longing sadness in their gut?

It's because this is where everything bad happens to you, Julian decided.

Every dying grandparent ends up there. Every painful broken arm, every helpless surgery, and every sick child. This is where they go.

The faces of the nurses were colder than the corridors; no eye contact and no smiles. This was where they worked, and where they witnessed death on a daily basis. To an extent, Julian understood it. He hardly showed up to an exorcism full of positivity and an eagerness to get to work. He showed up with his game face on, aware that death is a very real possibility lurking behind any poor decision.

He followed Jason Lyle into the lift. Jason was a police officer known to have a penchant for bizarre and baffling cases, ones that he normally brought the Sensitives into. It hadn't always been like that – in fact, Jason had solicited Julian's arrest over a year ago. But, having witnessed the truth of the supernatural forces attacking this world, he now sought their advice on a regular basis.

Julian held his hand out as the lift doors went to close, waiting for Derek to catch up. He took far longer than he did weeks ago – or even days ago. He looked to be deteriorating by the minute. His hair was growing back in a small mound after his last dose of chemotherapy, but his energy was not growing back as fast. He turned pale and out of breath, hobbling along on his walking stick, desperate not to be a burden in his unsuccessful attempt to catch up with the other two.

As Derek entered the lift and Julian allowed the doors to close, he studied Derek for a few moments. The sad truth was that Julian knew there was going to come a time when Derek would not be able to help him anymore and, whilst it had never been verbalised, he was fairly sure that Derek understood this too. But, until that day, Derek insisted that he was still an integral part of the paranormal hunting process – saying, "If anything's going to kill me, it'll be a demon, not a damn illness!"

As ever, Julian's mentor's words could not have been any closer to the truth.

With a sullen ping the lift doors parted and they stepped into the children's ward. At first, they walked through what seemed to be an inflated corridor – a passageway to the main ward, wide enough that it contained a row of beds on either side. This led them to a larger, square room with a succession of beds around the edges and a few lines of beds through the middle. Happy clowns and playful pictures of colourful fields adorned the curtains draped around the overcrowded succession of beds, but they only added a sense of irony to the morose and sombre mood of the wing. Julian imagined that this ward wouldn't have felt much different to Derek than the prison he had previously been trapped inside. People walked sombrely, without eye contact, desperate not to share their sorrow, helplessly confined to the sanctity of their beds and their cubicles.

That, Julian imagined, was why Derek was so adamant in not occupying the hospital bed he so sorely needed.

"Detective Inspector Jason Lyle," Jason introduced himself to a nearby nurse. "We're here investigating the death of Tommy Rowe."

The nurse's grim expression fell even lower.

"Right this way."

She led them to the corner of the larger room, where the far bed had been cordoned off by police tape and been further hidden by the drawn curtain. The beds around this police tape had recently been filled on Jason's confirmation that they were nearly done with the crime scene; he just wanted the thoughts of another set of people before it was completely cleared.

As they approached the crime scene, Jason tore down a strip of the tape and opened the curtain, allowing Julian and Derek inside. They stood and stared for a few moments.

The sheets themselves were a crusty red. The floor still held the remnants of the attack, and one would struggle to read the screens on the nearby machines, such was the mass of blood stains.

"Jesus," Julian unknowingly gasped.

"Yeah," Jason acknowledged.

"How many is that now?"

"We have the doctor, and this is the second child. Both with the same circumstance. The same problem."

"Remind me," Derek requested, his voice slow and weak.

"No evidence of an intruder, neither on CCTV nor by forensic analysis. No evidence of DNA but the boy's. But an attack that undoubtedly went on beyond the point of death – not one that could be attributed to suicide."

Derek feebly nodded. Every word seemed to fall on his ears at a slower pace. It took him a few minutes to fully comprehend and process the answer to his question, in which time Julian grew guiltily impatient.

"Why would a kid that young commit suicide anyway?" Julian pointed out. "It's... Wow. It's unusual."

"Yes, it is unusual; that's why I've recruited you."

"No, that's not what I mean. It's – the whole situation is unusual. We have no doubt from what we've seen so far that there is strong evidence to attribute this to something... more. It's just that this isn't typical of the type of assailant we are speaking of."

"What do you mean?"

Julian sighed, raising his hand to his cheek, which he stroked curiously.

"Just hypothesising here – but those who are close to death, such as a seriously sick child, are more vulnerable to seeing elements that exist beyond death. That suggests that a demon, or spirit – an entity, shall we say – is at play. It's just, demons aren't serial killers, so much as manipulators."

"It's a demon. Surely it would do whatever?"

"Yes, that would be true – but its capabilities would not extend to physical interaction as much as physical manipulation. A demon would normally guide a host to carry out its actions, which would leave the DNA of said host, or one would have thought. This... it's curious."

Jason's phone rang. He looked at it, and an expression of irritation swept over his face.

"I'll be right back," he said, and left.

Julian turned to Derek, who was lowering himself slowly into a chair in the corner of the room. He closed his eyes for a moment, gathering his energy.

"You all right?" Julian inquired.

"Fine," Derek replied.

"You know, you really need to check into a–"

"I'm not having this same argument again."

Julian sighed to keep cool, and decided to return focus to the scene at hand.

"So, what do you think?" Julian asked.

"This does appear to be some kind of entity."

"Well, there we have it. Just another day at the office. Playing with all the evil in the world."

Derek stared with a half-smile at Julian. Julian thought for a moment that this was his delayed reaction, then noticed the glint in his eye Derek always had when he was having a deep thought.

"What?"

"Such a cynic," Derek observed. "Always so desperate to attribute everything to evil."

"Well, don't you? What with everything we've seen, the true horrors, how can you not dwell on all the shittiness in this world? This world is crap. Stinking. And overfilled with evil and misery."

Derek leant his head back and closed his eyes, but did not lose the smile from his face.

"If I have one dying wish, before I go," he announced. "It's that I prove you wrong."

"Prove me wrong?"

"It's easy, when all you are exposed to is the sadness in the world, to believe that's all there is. You just have to remember sometimes to push that aside and see all the good it is concealing."

"Out of everyone I know, surely you have the most reason not to believe that."

Derek's grin widened. His eyes opened and fell on Julian's.

"And that, my good friend, is why I choose to."

Julian dropped his head.

As good as Derek's intentions were, he struggled to believe him. Yes, Julian was sure there was good in the world.

It's just that the child's bloodstains on the sheets before him suggested otherwise.

7

OSCAR BURST THROUGH THE DOOR WITH A JOVIAL SMILE GLUED upon his bright face. He had spent the day hunting for the perfect six-month anniversary/moving in together present for April, and had returned with a bracelet he was, at first, incredibly confident she would like. The journey home, however, had left him profusely doubtful, and he was desperate to get the moment of exchange over and done with.

He closed the door behind him and kicked his shoes off, calling hastily for her.

"April! April!"

Silence.

Having been caught up in his eager happiness, he had failed to notice the absence of light. Not a lamp was lit in the house, and it left him with a sense of foreboding building in the pit of his stomach, like a set of locusts setting up a wrestling match inside his belly.

Maybe she wasn't home?

But the door wasn't locked.

"April? Are you there?"

He warily edged through to the kitchen, looking around, switching the light on as he entered.

Nothing.

"April? Please answer me."

He edged through to the living room, and the sight of an ominous silhouette in the corner made him jump. After the initial shock he saw it was April, and turned the light on.

"April, what are you doing?"

He rushed over to her and put his hands on her arms. That's when he saw her face. Her wet eyes, her red cheeks, and her solemn expression pointed at the floor. Her body wasn't in the confident posture she normally sauntered through these rooms with, but instead had a morose slant, like a wilted flower or an expired piece of fruit.

"What is it?" Oscar insisted. He tried lifting her face, but she wouldn't budge. "Hey, come on. Happy six-month anniversary. Yeah? I got you something."

He took a big breath, readied himself for rejection, and withdrew the bracelet from his bag, presenting it to her. She greeted it with an immediate gasp, grabbing it off him, and lifting it to her eyes. She studied its gold plate and decorative indentations.

"You like it?"

"I – I love it."

Her hands dropped and her sombreness returned, as if she had just remembered something awful that meant the bracelet's charm wouldn't last.

Oscar grew abruptly fearful. Why was she so sad? He'd never seen her this sad before.

Then it struck him.

Is she going to break up with me?

His breathing quickened pace and his head rushed around a hundred responses, none of them good.

No. Don't be so pessimistic.

But in truth, he had already decided that she was not only going to break up with him, but for a man with far more muscles, intelligence, and a more generous penis size.

"April…"

"Oscar, I'm pregnant," she blurted out.

Oscar breathed a sigh of relief. His body untensed and his muscles relaxed.

She wasn't cheating.

She wasn't breaking up with him.

Everything was okay.

"Oh, phew," he unknowingly spoke.

"What?" April retorted, a face full of fury.

"Oh, no, I mean–"

Then it suddenly sunk over him, what she had just said.

Pregnant.

April.

Pregnant April.

Baby.

April pregnant baby.

"So…"

His first question was, *is it mine?* But his instinct told him that this was not the correct response.

He fought against words in his mind to form a coherent phrase. Finally, he relaxed, and allowed his true feelings to rise to the surface.

"That's… brilliant!"

"What?"

"That's… amazing. I mean, I know it's not planned, but… wow. I mean, I – I'm happy!"

"You're happy? Honestly?"

"Yes."

Oscar threw his hands around April and lifted her up – making sure not to groan as he did, as that made her insecure (he'd learnt that before) – and spun her around. It put a strain on his muscles that he didn't expect, despite her small, dainty disposition – but he didn't care. He regretted nothing. He was elated.

"Why?"

"What?"

"Why are you so happy, Oscar?"

"Because you – you are the love of my life. And I always dreamt of this eventually. Sure, it may be a little sooner than we thought–"

"A *lot* sooner."

"–but, you know what, screw it. I love you. I love us. And if this gives me something else to love, well then, I guess I'll just have to find the room."

April smiled quizzically at him. It was as if he'd just reminded her of all the millions of reasons that she loved him. She flung her arms around his neck and pushed a passionate, heartfelt kiss against his lips.

"I love you, Oscar."

"I love you, April."

He held her tight as those words sank through his thoughts like a hand brushing through a gentle wave: *I'm going to be a daddy. I'm going to have a baby with April.*

And he knew, in that precious moment, that nothing could take away that fiery spark he felt pumping through him that told him this was the woman his life had been created for.

8

'BEAT THOSE HOLIDAY BLUES.'

'Five Fun Fat-Burning Facts.'

'Organise Your Clear-out Like a Pro.'

As Oscar thumbed through the pages of the *Good House-keeping* magazine, he decided it was not for him. He didn't find that he particularly had any post-Christmas blues, nor did he find a longing desire to burn lots of fat. If anything, he was a bit thin and scrawny, and he could do with adding some. Any t-shirt he wore was either too baggy or, if tight, only outlined his strange boniness.

He threw the magazine back onto the pile and sifted through the rest of the reading material available in the waiting room of the obstetrician's office – a word he had learnt the previous day. When April had requested he go with her to the obstetrician's, he assumed it was some ridiculous magic show at the local theatre. After April had appeared extremely disappointed and overly-sensitive at his detest of the idea, he googled it on his phone, and returned to the room to make a swift and much needed apology.

So there he sat, in the waiting room. Reading the women's monthlies piled upon the table next to him.

Cosmopolitan. Red. Prime. OK! InStyle.

Why are all these magazines for women?

He sighed and turned away. Honestly, did they not think men ever sat in a waiting room? Yet he could not think of a single waiting room he'd been in that had a copy of *Empire* or *Sci-Fi Now*. It was as if there was some giant conspiracy where the magazine suppliers of waiting rooms were trying to prohibit men from the whole waiting experience.

"What are you thinking about?" April asked him, with a cheeky smile on her face.

Oscar wondered whether to be honest or not.

"I was thinking about how much I'm looking forward to our first scan," he replied, prompting a loving smile from April's beaming face. He pushed the thoughts of magazine conspiracies from his mind and took her hand firmly in his.

"Do you have any idea how far along you actually are?" Oscar asked. "I mean, I know we're bound to find out, I just wondered."

"I don't know."

Oscar nodded. He looked around the waiting room. They were, without doubt, the youngest couple there. Not only that, but the only couple without a rounded pregnant belly. There were four other women, three of which had a man next to them, and a few who had toddlers playing with some waiting room toys, having found something evidently far more inter-esting than the collection of women's monthlies. Some of the men had facial hair; Oscar could barely grow a substantial amount of whiskers to resemble a moustache. One man sat in a suit, looking very business-like. The other had hair that was partially grey.

I'm twenty. I'm not that old...

"Hey, April," Oscar subtly whispered, "I feel, like, really…"

"Young?"

"Yeah."

"Totally. It's freaking me out."

Oscar held her hand tighter.

"It's fine. We're adults. It's cool."

Adults.

Yeah, I'm an adult. As if.

Oscar wasn't sure he knew of many other parents who bought tickets for the midnight showing of the new *Star Wars* movie, or who had an impressive comic book collection that took up two bookcases.

April's hand suddenly seized. As Oscar turned to her, he could see her face grimacing.

"What's the matter?" he asked.

"Nothing," April insisted. A rumble of thunder echoed outside the window. "Nothing, I just–"

She abruptly convulsed, grabbing hold of her belly with both hands as she did. Oscar instinctively put his arm around her, but became distracted by the ensuing moans that then came from each of the other pregnant women in the room. Seconds after April's pain, each mother-to-be grabbed hold of their belly, with the same grimace on their face.

April's tension relieved slightly and her arms loosened.

"God, April, are you–"

Before he could say another word, she grabbed onto her belly again, moaning and writhing in agony. Seconds after, the rest of the women followed in perfect unison. A room full of women clutching onto pregnant bellies, and their partners checking if they were okay.

Oscar found it strange. But he thought nothing further of it, and put his arm around April.

Her body loosened once more, and she relaxed.

"Are you all right?" he asked.

"Yeah. Yeah, I'm fine. Just a bit of pain."

"April Cristine?" came the sound of the obstetrician.

April stood up, grabbed her bags, and Oscar had to hurry to follow her into the room.

"Hello, I'm Doctor Janet Stave," the woman introduced herself. She was a portly black woman with a kind face and piercing green eyes. A long, white coat hung open, and she had more jewellery on her arms than needed. Beside her dangling earrings was a comforting, reassuring smile, and the friendliness one would hope for in the situation. "You must be April, which means you must be Oscar."

She shook their hands, and allowed April sit upright on the bed. Oscar took the seat next to April, still keeping hold of her hand.

"Is everything okay then?"

"Yeah, I've just had a few pains in the waiting room, but beside that, fine."

"Okay, well it's perfectly normal to feel a bit of discomfort, but we'll check you out and make sure everything's okay. Are you all right to lean back for me and we'll do your scan?"

April reluctantly laid back, allowing Doctor Stave to lift April's top over her belly and rub some jelly over her navel. It was cold at first, and made April shudder, but she kept hold of Oscar's hand and did her best to quell her nerves.

"Okay, are you ready?"

April nodded, though her eyes screamed terror. Oscar wondered what it was she was worried about. The pregnancy had been unprecedented, yes, but surely she couldn't be letting that cast a negative mindset over the whole process.

"It's okay," Oscar told April. "We're going to see the baby on the screen, and you'll see, it's going to be great."

April nodded again, without any conviction or certainty.

Doctor Stave turned the screen toward them.

"Right, if you just have a look at the screen," she instructed. "You will be able to see–"

Just as Oscar turned his attention toward the monitor to see the image of his child the screen flickered, and the image became a series of wavy lines.

"Oh," Doctor Stave said. "I don't really know what's happening."

She gave the screen a tap and waited. It continued to disrupt, showing squiggly absent lines, as if it was a very old television unable to get a reception.

"This has never happened before," Doctor Stave told them. "I'll tell you what, I'll see if I can get it to print."

She tapped a few keys on the keyboard and switched off the flickering screen. She reached for the printer, which came to life. The whirs of the rolling paper sounded without issue. Then, as soon as it came to ink being placed upon the paper, the printer began to wheeze and cough. The paper jammed, causing a screech that only grew louder and more painful, as if someone had grabbed hold of a cat and squeezed it until it squealed.

"This is really strange," Doctor Stave admitted. "Please just give me a minute. I'll go and see if someone can help."

As she left, April turned her wounded expression toward Oscar. He could see a disguised tear sticking to the corner of her eye.

"Do you think it's a sign?" she asked, her voice weak and worried.

"A sign of what? Don't be silly, equipment malfunctions sometimes. It's all going to be okay."

"But, what if–"

"No," Oscar insisted, placing his hands firmly around hers and forcing her eyes to look into his. "I need you to stop this right now. Stop the worrying about nothing. This is all going to be okay."

"You think?"

"I think? April, I promise." He loosened a hand and ran it affectionately down her cheek. "Everything is going to be perfect."

9

YEARS AGO – HELL, MAYBE EVEN MONTHS AGO – DEREK WOULD have remained by that empty, blood-stained bed and debated with Jason and Julian until his voice grew hoarse.

He knew, however, and very much against his own reluctance, that his time for such contributions was at an end. He did not have the energy to provide the tenacity needed for a hearty debate. It wasn't just the illness, it was in his bones. His heart felt weaker, and he felt tired at such stressful jobs. He wouldn't have been able to join in the conversation for long without falling asleep during the most poignant part of the debate.

No, he knew when he wasn't needed. So he found himself using his sturdy walking stick to guide his aching bones away from the hypothesising and discussing and wondering that Jason and Julian were engaging in to find a place to rest elsewhere in the children's ward whilst he waited.

Maybe he could even get a head start back to the car. He chuckled to himself, as he imagined himself getting a half-hour advantage that they overtook within minutes.

He paused by the water fountain, reaching out for a paper

cup. Even the action of leaning his walking stick against the wall and reaching out his feeble arm took him more energy than he could expend without finding an ache engraining into his bones with a prominence he couldn't ignore.

He hated feeling useless. But the one thing he hated more was feeling like a burden.

"What are you talking about?" came an inquisitive voice.

Derek slowly rotated his head toward a nearby bed, where a young boy's face stared at him.

"Excuse me?" Derek said.

"You were muttering something. What is it?"

"Ah." Derek smiled. The approach of a child was always so direct and without embarrassment. If only we could all be so bold. "I was thinking about something that made me sad."

"What was it?"

"Well. That would take a while to explain."

"I'm not going anywhere."

Derek grinned. He admired the boy's tenacity.

"Okay," Derek decided. "Do you mind if I sit?"

The boy shrugged.

Derek finished his water, retrieved his walking stick, and made the long walk of a few metres to the chair beside the boy's bed.

"You haven't much hair, like me," the boy pointed out, staring at Derek's post-treatment prickles perching atop his scalp. The boy, too, had an absence of hair, only he looked to be more in the midst of it. The only break from the paleness of his face were the prominent black bags beneath his eyes.

"I do. That's because I'm ill, as well."

"Are you really?"

"Yes. My name is Derek, by the way. What is yours?"

"Charlie."

"Charlie. Wonderful name. How old are you, Charlie?"

"Ten."

"Ten. What a lovely age. And do you have a close friend, Charlie? Like a best friend."

The boy pointed at a girl asleep in the bed next to his.

"Her name is Joanna."

"Joanna. A lovely name too." Derek paused to take a moment to gather his thoughts. "Well, Charlie, to answer your question. I had a best friend once, but he died many, many years ago. Since then I have been doing the best I can to pay respect to his memory. To help people. Only now, I can't."

"Why not?"

"Well, because I'm either too old, or too ill. Or both."

Charlie looked down at his fidgeting hands, nodding.

"I understand how you feel. I wish I could have helped Tommy. But I couldn't."

"Who's Tommy?"

Charlie looked confused at the question.

"You know who Tommy is."

"Sorry, Charlie, but I don't."

"You came in with those two other men, didn't you? The ones who have gone to see Tommy's bed?"

Ah.

Derek dropped his head in a moment of understanding.

"I see. And were you and Tommy close?"

Charlie eagerly nodded.

"I'm sorry, Charlie. It's never nice to lose someone we care about. Especially when they are ill."

"He didn't die because he was ill."

"What makes you say that?"

"Because I saw it."

Derek leant forward.

"What did you see, Charlie?"

"The thing that killed him. We've all seen it. Well, all of us who have been here long enough to see it."

"And what does it look like, Charlie?"

Charlie looked fearfully into Derek's eyes. His lips remained tightly sealed, and his eyes widened into a worried stare.

"Charlie, I can help you. What did it look like?"

Charlie shook his head, keeping his lips closed as tight as he could.

"Charlie, what does it–"

"Derek."

Derek turned and saw Jason and Julian waiting behind him, indicating that it was time to leave. He turned back to Charlie and gave him a sincere, heartfelt smile.

"It was nice to meet you, Charlie. I hope to see you again soon."

He nodded at the child and followed the other two out of the building. As he struggled to even remain in the shadow of the other two's hefty pace, ignored as they engaged in heated discussion, his mind remained on Charlie, and what the boy had witnessed.

10

It was a familiar sight to Julian. Many books with many dusty covers laid open upon a desk, sending powdery clouds into his twitching nose. They were sporadically placed but precisely opened on marked pages that referred to demons with a focus on children.

Julian glanced at Jason with a sly smirk. To him, opening these ancient books, reading their overbearing language, and sifting through their hefty pages was a normal part of the process of identifying who he, or the other Sensitives, were going to have to do battle with. To Jason, this was the first time sifting through these books about demons and the occult. Jason gave the same perplexed looks at the browned pages he thumbed through as Julian had when Derek had first introduced him to them.

"Any ideas?" Julian prompted, standing behind Jason with a knowing expression.

"I – this is – well…"

"You can say no."

Jason returned Julian's grin.

"These books are beyond what I imagined. Does all this

stuff really exist? I mean, these many demons, these many types of ghosts, it all, just, seems…"

"A bit farfetched?"

Jason nodded.

"Tell me about it."

The front door opened and within moments, Oscar and April had burst into the room. Happy smiles spread across their faces, their hands entwined with each other's, barely able to rip their eyes from each other. It made Julian want to gag. It was like seeing a younger sister with an irritating boyfriend.

"Great," Julian said. "Now the happy couple are here, we can get some input."

"Sorry we're late," Oscar offered. The grin stuck to his face spoke nothing of apology whatsoever.

"Well, if you're done touching each other up and giggling like toddlers, a child has died."

April's smile ceased. She bit her lip. She looked up at Julian with those eyes of vulnerability he saw whenever she was scared or worried about something. Those same eyes he had seen when he first approached her when she was living on the streets.

"We kind of have some news," April announced. "I mean, I know this is important, so we'll be really quick."

"What?" Julian barked.

"I'm – well, see…"

"She's pregnant!" Oscar interjected.

Julian felt as if he'd just been smacked in the face with a large metal rod. At first he couldn't believe it. He thought it was part of some ridiculous, ill-timed joke. Then, as he saw their awaiting expressions peering back it him, the realisation that this news was true washed over him like a bucket of ice.

April? Pregnant?

Oscar? A dad.

It was ridiculous.

They are just kids.

"Well?" April prompted. "Aren't you going to say anything?"

Julian could see it in her eyes. The need for his approval. The need for his reassuring words to tell her it was going to be okay. She needed him to say something to comfort her, to calm her on this inevitable path of destruction she had set herself upon.

But he couldn't.

He had no words.

"It's marvellous news," came a voice from the doorway. As the owner of the soft declaration of joy hobbled further, he managed to reach the nearest chair, planting himself upon it and breathing a sigh of relief. "I told you good would still prevail."

"Derek." Oscar smiled widely. "It's great to see you."

"It's great to see you, too," Derek said. "This is wonderful. A child! You must tell us all the news. How far along are you?"

"Actually, if you lot don't mind," Julian interrupted, "We have two dead kids and a dead doctor on our hands, with a likely imminent death pretty soon. So maybe we can save all this for later."

"Julian?" April said. "Why are you being like this?"

"Like what?" Julian snapped. "What do you want from me? My blessing? Good luck. To the pair of you. It's going to be lovely."

He turned his grimace back to the numerous open books awaiting his attention.

"Julian–"

"Look – if you are quite done, we do actually have a job to do. Like finding out who this demon is."

"You don't need to," came Derek's meek voice. "I can tell you."

"What?" Julian scoffed, bowed his head and rubbed his

sinus, doing all he could to avoid the frustration pent up inside from bursting out.

"I have fought this thing before."

"How could you possibly know that?"

"Oh, I know. Trust me."

"Right." Julian slammed closed all the books, swivelled to Derek, and lurched his body forward with his hands on his hips. "Do go on. Please. Save us the hours we have already pissed away researching."

"The demon's name is Lamia."

"Lamia?"

"Yes. Lamia. A demon of Greek origin, said to be the mistress of a god, once a beautiful queen of Libya. She possessed a young girl from Portugal I once knew. In Scotland."

"It possessed a Portuguese girl in Scotland?" Julian scathingly repeated. "And what is it about this demon that makes you think it's her?"

Derek stroked his chin, studying Julian's defiant face.

"Because this girl killed, and ate, twelve children. Just before I watched her throw herself off a cliff."

"…Oh."

THEN

11

THE CRUNCH OF LEAVES FOUGHT AGAINST THE SOLES OF Martin's feet. The further he walked the sparser they became, replaced by wet soil. Eventually, the wetness mixed with speckles of blood, and Martin ceased his searching.

Beside his feet were two eyes, wide and still, upon the pale face of Madelina's corpse. The hair brushed over her mouth didn't blow outwards from her breath, nor did her chest rise or her fingers flinch. The moonlight barely even reflected in her pupils, such was the lack of life that consumed her.

Martin knelt beside her. Reached a hand out. Brushed the hair off her face. Traced his fingers down her neck, which had grown so stiff, and so cold. They travelled further downwards, gently running down her chest until they landed upon her belly, home to a child that was a month off being born.

He rested his hand there.

He felt nothing.

No bumps. No movement. Not even a gurgle.

Not a single recognition from the baby of its father.

Martin bowed his head. Allowed his eyes to rest shut.

He made the decision never to tell Derek that it was his

child. He'd introduced Madelina as a friend in trouble, believing that his mentor would know the best thing to do. Her symptoms were terrifying – with the lust for meat and bizarre behaviour she was exhibiting, it was as if the demon had targeted Martin personally.

He shook his head. Forced tears from his eyes.

Who was he kidding?

Of course it was a personal attack.

After the wars he and Derek had waged, the demons they had defeated, the lengths they had gone to so they could keep hell quiet and banish evil from the earth. Had they really expected no retaliation?

He allowed his eyes to flutter open, fixing them on hers. They looked back, but they didn't. It was a strange feeling. To see someone staring at him, knowing there was nothing behind that stare.

Even in death, her eyes retained the unmistakable vulnerability they'd held in life. She was so strong, a dominative force, someone who would not take shit off anyone. But beneath that, behind the exterior of her strong feminine character, was a scared voice. He could see it. No one else could, but he could.

He hated Derek. In that moment, he hated him. Despised him. It was his fault. It was all his fault.

Derek had insisted. No exorcism. She was too weak. Too pregnant.

That was his child.

Derek was not to know, but that was Martin's child.

A rustle of leaves from behind him disturbed his melancholy state. He shook it off.

He had a job to do.

He stood. Turned. Faced the direction of the quiver of leaves.

Shadows brushed the trees so faintly that a blink would have robbed him of the sight.

"I know you are there," he said. "And I know who you are."

He withdrew his cross from his pocket. Gently kissed it. Held it firmly. Gripping it. Clutching it.

Madelina was gone.

Martin was not here for her.

He was here to clean up Derek's mess.

When she had jumped, she had banished the demon from her body. But that did not mean it was not banished from this earth.

In the far blackness of the bushes two piercing red eyes appeared, then blinked back to nothing.

"You want me to be angry," Martin observed. "You want this to take the better of me. I know that. I feel it."

He paused. Held his head at an angle. Removed any emotion from his body.

"But I am the son of heaven, and you will not beat me. Nor will you intimidate me."

He stepped forward with a confident stride. His arm decisively rose as he presented the cross in the direction of the disturbances.

"Reveal yourself, you filthy dominion of hell."

The rustles punched leaves into the air and fluttered the branches of the trees. This happened again. And again. And again. Until eventually, bursts of leaves feverishly pumped into the air across Martin's eyesight as if being fired from a machine, painting the dark night before him with red and green flickers.

"You think that's going to scare me?" Martin mocked. "Throwing a bunch of leaves?"

Enough.

Time to rid this world of this child-eating monstrosity of the underworld.

"The spirit of the Lord is upon me," Martin began, holding his cross out before him. "I address you, Lamia, demoness of hell, as the one anointed to preach the gospel and preach deliverance to the captives. I preach the acceptable year of the Lord."

A screech shook the trees, the sound like a combination of a crow and a woman in peril. Birds fled the trees in which they nested, sensing the impending danger.

Martin was not scared. He was perturbed. But not because of this demon.

This was Derek's job.

And he was having to do it.

"For whosoever shall call upon the name of the Lord shall be saved," Martin persisted. "And I call upon the name of the Lord. And I am saved."

A ball of flames burst from the cross, firing into five corners of a pentagon that floated as his defence.

"Forgive me my sins, cleanse me, and give me the power to banish this demon."

Martin felt it. The strength. The power. It surged through him, an electrical charge pumping through his veins.

"Reveal yourself."

The screech repeated itself, this time deafening, but not deterring Martin. Its face appeared as an apparition, the face of a woman, beautiful yet twisted, an uncomfortably appealing haze. Beneath its naked chest was a snakeskin waist, above the tail of a serpent.

It shook its head with a cackle.

Martin knew this wasn't over. That this demon was part of the devil's plan. That its revenge would come back.

"Be gone," Martin spoke softly, trying not to think of the deceased pregnant woman lying behind his feet. "Be gone."

She faded away into a smoky haze.

One might be forgiven for thinking that Martin had won.

But, as he slowly twisted back toward the body that lay behind him, he knew it was not over. It was never over. The demon may have left, but its mission had been completed. It had torn him and Derek apart.This final appearance was just its mocking visage tormenting him.

As if to say, "Until the next time."

Martin didn't blame it.

And, as he lay by Madelina's sweet head, all he could think about was the man he did blame.

NOW

12

A FLICKERING AMBER GLOW OF THREE CANDLES ILLUMINATED THE bedroom. One placed on Derek's bedside table, one on the desk opposite, and one on the windowsill. He liked being in a room lit only by candles. He told himself that it was because the light was natural, and it made him feel calm and serene. In truth, it was a habit he'd become used to as a way of detecting a supernatural attack; with the fights he had fought, he had become a vulnerable target, and if the candles brawled against a breeze in a room with a closed window and secure door, it would give him the first indication of an imminent presence.

As he sat on the edge of his bed, he ran his hands through his hair, which was damp from sweat. The process of walking upstairs had taken far more energy than he had to expend – he needed a few moments to mentally prepare for the energy it would take to lie down and pull the duvet over himself.

"Right," announced Julian as he barged in, placing a glass of water on the bedside table.

He opened the drawer and took out a pill box, arranging three pills from separate sections in his hands. He held them toward Derek.

"Here they are," Julian said in a thoroughly business-like fashion. "Do you want the glass of water?"

Derek took a moment to look at Julian's partially lit face. He was often short-tempered and snappy, such was his way; but there seemed to be something else. Something cold in the way he was conducting himself.

"Yes, please," Derek eventually answered, taking the pills from Julian's hand. He placed the first in his mouth, took the glass of water from Julian, and gulped it down.

"Good night then," Julian curtly grunted.

"Julian, wait."

Julian paused by the door.

"What?"

"Sit down."

Julian shook his head in a disdainful manner, huffing with annoyance.

"Derek, it's been a long day. I really don't have time."

"Don't have time for an ill man who taught you how to do the job you are so busy doing? Please, just sit."

As Derek took his second pill, Julian hesitated. Derek sure did have a way with words, and he knew it. What's more, he knew Julian, and he knew what to say to persuade him.

Julian gave another huff as he threw himself on the chair beside the door, slouching as if he were a teenager waiting outside the headmaster's office.

"What?" he barked.

Derek took the final pill and finished the water, placing the glass gently upon the bedside table.

"What's bothering you?" Derek asked, slowly and calmly.

"What's bothering me? We have dead kids, and probably more if we don't get moving, and we're pissing about, making me sit and listen to another lecture that I am bloody well sure is coming."

Derek nodded. Thought. Took his time.

"No," he decided. "No. That's not it. Tell me what's really bothering you."

"What?" Julian demanded, sitting forward, fixing his seething eyes on Derek.

"The way you spoke to April, to Oscar. I know you've had your differences with Oscar, but he came up big for us when we needed him. And April, I know how deeply you care for her. So why react like that?"

"This is pointless, Derek, I'm not going to–"

"Not going to what? Admit that you were unkind?"

"Damn it, Derek, they are children. Kids having kids. What do you want me to say? Them having a baby is bloody ridiculous. There. Said it."

"Right, fair enough. Now you've said it to me, you can keep it to yourself."

Julian glared at Derek. Not just stared, or gave him evil eyes – intensely glared. Peering his annoyance deep into Derek's retina.

"I can keep it to myself?" Julian repeated in a low-pitched growl.

"Yes. You can," Derek confirmed. "Because I'd bet that those two – being kids, as you refer to them – are bloody terrified right now. And they could do with some support. And that support needs to come from the one they look up to most." He pointed at Julian's heart. "You."

A lingering absence of speech hovered in the air, settling like a bomb exploding on the ground and rising into dust. Julian let it simmer, let his irritation grow. Derek could see Julian's thoughts working, could see Julian going from one annoyed retort to another. Trying to decide which vile insult or comeback to fire back with.

"You want to know what's really bothering me?" Julian spat.

"I truly do."

"You. You, who are so ill you shouldn't be anywhere but a

71

hospital – but because you're so stubborn, you place the burden on *me* to look after you. Don't get me wrong, I have no problem doing it – you just have no idea what effort it takes. Because I have to run this business, solve a murder, defeat a child-killing demon, then force-feed you your sodding pills. And then I have to sit here and be subjected to a lecture about my manners and treatment of others, before you then go onto your incessant rambling about how good will always prevail, how good will go on, how good will do this, do that, yada yada yada. It's bullshit. All of it, it's bullshit."

Julian stood, unmoved. Hovering between Derek and the door. A flicker of apology for his outburst passed over Julian's eyes with the movement of the candle, then it was gone.

"Goodnight," he spoke, then left, shutting the door behind him.

Derek bowed his head.

Was he placing too much of a burden on Julian? Maybe this was a cry for help. Maybe the stress was getting to him. Maybe the pregnancy meant that the two people who were meant to be helping him were now going to be otherwise engaged, and this meant that the weight on Julian's shoulders was only getting bigger.

Either way, Julian couldn't know.

He couldn't know about the nine months Derek spent trying to rid that demon from Madelina. About how futile it was.

About how the demon's intentions were entirely to inflict this pain upon Derek. To find an innocent female victim, put something in that victim, something the victim would protect against even Derek, and let it consume that dreaded woman.

Madelina was lucky. She killed herself before she could release the demon's spawn upon the world.

What if it was happening all over again?

No.

Julian had many burdens, but this burden of knowledge was not for him. Not whilst he was in this state.

It belonged to someone who believed that this thing could still be defeated but good. By hope. By the same tools they had used and prayed for in every exorcism Derek had partaken in.

Derek decided, then and there, that Lamia's true nature would stay with him.

That was, until the day he had to fight it.

If he lived that long.

(6 MONTHS)

13

JULIAN SEARCHED THE SHELVES FOR WHAT MUST HAVE BEEN AT least the fifteenth time. Maybe even the twentieth. But it felt like the hundredth.

His thumb ran past the same rough edges of old, brown-paged sheets. The scuffed leather binding of ancient literature pushed out spurts of dust as he flicked past numerous titles adorning the sturdy shelf.

The Occult a History: 1400 to 1600.

The Demonologist's Handbook.

Exorcism: Alive and Well in the Twentieth Century.

None of these damn books had a single mention of Lamia. Not a drawing, reference, or even a mention in passing. It was like the demon either didn't exist, or all knowledge of it had been wiped off the earth.

Julian didn't even know why he was bothering.

Derek was once a great man. He was as good a mentor as Julian could hope for, and had taught him everything he knew. He was a legendary exorcist, having fought in the biggest war that mankind would never know it faced. He had saved thousands of souls, punished more demons than he was able to take

77

stock of, and had saved more lives than most could achieve in a lifetime.

But that wasn't Derek anymore.

Derek was ill. Desperately, painfully ill. He wouldn't admit it, but his health was deteriorating by the day. What was once an astute, well-spoken, always smartly dressed, educated man was now a man who could barely walk across a room without needing to sit down.

The burden Derek placed on Julian day to day was more intense than the man could realise. Derek insisted he didn't need a hospital, saying he had no problem dying on his own terms – but what about those who cared for him? Those who were then left to do an inadequate job of what a qualified doctor should be doing?

It wasn't fair. And Julian was struggling to retain patience.

He dropped his weight into the nearest chair and slouched. He huffed. Then he huffed again.

He was tired. Exasperated. Irritated. Exhausted. Drained. Weary. Mentally full.

It was like someone just kept shovelling more and more into his head, filling it with stress, filling it with more burdens to worry about, then squeezed the top of his skull on tight and stapled it shut until nothing would be able to escape its bursting contents.

Dead children.

Derek.

A demon that didn't seem to exist.

But why would Derek claim it was Lamia if that demon didn't exist?

Why would Derek claim he'd had experience with this demon?

Why would he say anything?

Because he was delusional. It was the only explanation.

The illness had pushed to his mind. Convinced him of

things. Twisted the truth until it wrapped around itself so many times that it became convoluted, and there was no awareness as to what the truth was anymore.

It wasn't that Derek was lying.

But that he was not the man he was.

Julian dropped his head to his palm, shaking it to himself.

How could he be so curt?

The man Derek had been. The things he had done.

Julian wouldn't know any of this, be anything of the person he was, if it weren't for the effort and energy Derek had put into not only training him, convincing him, and moulding him – but finding him in the first place.

He hadn't even known what a Sensitive was.

No.

Mustn't doubt Derek.

Not him. Not that man. Not the one guy Julian respected.

He leapt to his feet, projecting himself back to the hefty cupboard. It took up the entire wall of Derek's study and was at least three books deep. It was a large collection, but that would make sense – Derek had, after all, been collecting these works his entire life.

He dragged his fingers across the next few spines.

Demons: An Intermediate's Guide.

How to Find the Truth – Demon or Delusion?

Modern Demons in a Modern World.

Titles he was familiar with.

All titles he had used at some point. All titled he'd subjected himself to for numerous hours slaving away at their words, reading them until they became jumbled nonsense falling through his mind. Read them until the words didn't even look like words anymore, but mystical shapes forming unfamiliar patterns that only highlighted how much there was to be known, yet how little of it he knew.

He could remember almost every word.

There had never been any mention of Lamia amongst any of them. He was sure of it.

He could ask Derek. Ask for more information. Ask to be directed to the right book.

But what was the point?

Time to be honest with myself.

It was bollocks, wasn't it?

All of it.

Just the ramblings of a fading mind. When a brain with such a mass of intelligence begins to lose its grip on reality, that intelligence only makes it worse. An unwise man would have little to delude themselves with. A genius would have so much information to fire through their mind, they would be bound to lose the ability to comprehend it, make sense of it, or to create the right links.

No.

Time to look elsewhere.

Julian would take care of Derek as best he could. He would be as faithful to his mentor as his mentor had been to him.

As for the nonsensical ramblings, he would do no more than nod along.

It was time for Julian to take over.

He was the one who must lead the Sensitives without help or guidance.

The burden was now to fall upon him.

14

A NERVOUS ENERGY BATTERED ITS WINGS AROUND OSCAR'S stomach. He straightened his shirt. His cuffs. His collar. Smoothed his hair backwards. Fidgeted with his hands. Anything to keep himself occupied.

To say his relationship with his parents had been rocky would be like saying his relationship with Julian was full of brotherly love. Before he'd met April and discovered his abilities as a Sensitive, he'd left school at sixteen and worked in the local supermarket. This was fine for him, but to his parents, who had bestowed ambitions of university upon him since he was old enough to comprehend what further education was, this was a grave disappointment. They had reminded him every day when he returned from work that this was not where he should be; he had just never had ambition to do anything else. That all changed once he pursued paranormal investigation and found a career he was passionate about – after which, he'd thought they would be proud.

If anything, they had stung him with more disappointment than they had before.

They were interested in what they termed 'educated

careers': teacher, accountancy, engineering, advertising, pharmaceuticals. Not what they had described as, "Hocus pocus nonsense," upon the announcement that he had a new, exciting career.

This had prompted him to move out a few months ago, which had led to him more recently settling in a new home with April. His contact with them since his moving had been minimal. Greeting cards, a text message on a birthday, stopping over when it was a larger family gathering – but nothing where they spent a substantial amount of time in each other's company.

It seemed that the announcement of an imminent grandchild had changed this. They wanted to make amends. And that started with a family dinner where they would meet the soon-to-be mother of his child.

He could just imagine what their judgemental impression would be upon meeting this woman. They would see the purple-dyed hair, the tattoos of Tim Burton characters on her arm, the baggy jeans – and they would instantly despise her, before they had gotten to know the beautiful, kind-hearted, wonderful human being that lay beneath. This punky image was what had first attracted him to her, and he loved it. He dreaded that his parents wouldn't.

"What's the matter?" April asked as they stood before his parents' front door. "You're sweating."

"I know. I'm just, y'know… mentally preparing myself."

"For what? Knocking on the door?"

Oscar turned to April, his face overcome with fear.

"Jeeze," April exclaimed. "I didn't even see you this scared when you were facing a prison full of ghosts."

"I just want you to know, whatever they say or do, please, just, don't take it personally."

She placed her arms around him.

"I love you, Oscar. And I've got skin thicker than anything.

I'm more study than a Snickers bar."

"A Snickers bar?"

"Yep. I compared myself to a chocolate bar. And what of it?"

Oscar couldn't help but chuckle. He leant his forehead against hers. A gesture that had come to be special to them. A source of comfort they gave each other whenever they needed to make sure they knew they weren't alone.

"Well, you are nutty," Oscar joked.

April sniggered sarcastically.

"Now knock on the door," she prompted. "Come on."

Oscar nodded – more to himself than to her, as if preparing for the actions he was about to undertake – and turned to face the door. He stretched his arm out and placed four firm knocks against the wooden barricade between him and his elders.

Shortly after, they opened it. They held out their arms and greeted their son with an eager hug, then shook his girlfriend's hands with enthusiasm and energy he hadn't expected.

They were whisked inside and sat in the living room, where his dad made them a cup of tea and regaled them with stories of how the decorating of the room had gone wrong. They laughed. Oscar began to relax.

As the evening continued, they keenly questioned April about what they did and where she came from. She answered, and their prejudice toward his occupation had either gone, or was well disguised. Oscar's nerves faded with the setting of the evening sun outside, and before he knew it they were having a happy tea, engaging in willing conversation.

"So do you earn much from this business?" his dad asked April. "I mean, from your clients."

"Well, it depends on the client, really," April answered, smiling at Oscar's mother as she placed a plate of chicken and vegetables in front of her. "Thank you."

"How so?" his dad continued.

"Well, I mean, the wealth of the client is a definite factor.

We won't ask for money that they can't afford. Generally, we ask for a contribution toward our living, rather than a flat fee. After we finish and have helped them, they are usually so grateful that they try and shove as much money on us as they can. Sometimes they are even too generous, and we have to tell them to just give us what they are able, not what they want."

"Fascinating," his dad said, cutting a piece of chicken off the bone. "Really, fascinating."

"Do you find it rewarding?" his mum asked, then placed a scoop of vegetables on her spoon and directed them into her mouth.

"Oh, God yeah. I mean, it's tough. Particularly when we have to tell people there is nothing supernaturally occurring and they, you know, just need a doctor." His parents chuckled. "But when we do actually manage to succeed with a real case, it's rewarding to see the difference you have made to their lives."

Pleased that the conversation was flowing smoothly without his aid, Oscar cut a small amount of chicken and placed it in his mouth, ensuring he ate with his mouth closed. Their son or not, his parents were very middle-class people, and he did not want to seem rude with his table manners. It felt as if his relationship with them was repairable, and they were trying really hard; maybe he had to as well.

"So, tell us more about the baby," said his mum. "How far along are you?"

"Three months."

"And have you thought of any names yet?"

"Not really." April looked vaguely at Oscar. "We're still kind of dealing with the shock of it, I guess."

"Well, I bet. It must have come as quite a surprise. I remember when we had Oscar, we–"

A sudden, uncomfortable silence ensued.

Oscar stopped chewing. What had happened? Things were going so well? Why had…

He looked at April.

She had sunk her face to the level of her plate and dug her teeth into the side of the chicken, then ripped it off with her teeth like a lion feeding on a deer. She swung her head downwards again, sinking her teeth into the dead bird's flesh and ripping it away from the bone with such ferocity and such a large quantity, that it ended up poking between her lips as she chewed.

Oscar was astonished. If he ate his morning cereal with a slight opening in his mouth she would treat him as if he had just kicked her in the face and pissed on the table. Now, here she was, ravaging her meat like a hungry animal.

He had never seen her act in such a way.

"April…" he prompted.

She ignored him. Either that, or she didn't hear. She was too engrossed with grappling her teeth into the meat, engaging in a wrestling match between her and the bone, seeing who could win the most chicken.

"April," Oscar said again, a little louder.

Nothing.

She merely rotated the chicken – with her mouth, no less; her hands were securely on her lap – and devoured the other side with equal intensity.

Oscar looked to his parents, who were staring at this previously polite young woman, unsure what to do with their eyes. Do they stare? Do they look away? Do they comment? Ignore it? Demand her to leave?

It took her two more eager bites to rip away the remaining flesh. With sauce smeared across her cheeks, she picked up her cutlery and continued to eat her vegetables with the grace of a saint – never loading them up too highly, and munching with her mouth closed.

"Sorry?" she said, as if snapping out of a trance. "What did you say?"

"April," Oscar said. Once she looked at him, he pointed to his cheeks as an indication to clean hers.

"Oh, sorry, did I get some on me?" she asked, picking up her napkin and wiping her mouth. "What was your question?"

"Erm, yes, well," his father attempted to continue. "Where was I? Ah, yes. When we had Oscar."

"Well, I, uh," his mother tried to take over. "Yes. It was quite a shock. We were wanting children, but not quite yet."

The conversation resumed, and no more uncharacteristically rude gestures or actions were made. Oscar watched April intently, trying to figure her out, trying to understand what on earth had caused her bizarre actions. It was like he was on a hidden camera show, and someone was going to burst out any moment and reveal that it was all a ruse. A con, and they really did have him going.

But no one burst out. No comment was made, and she barely acknowledged it.

As the evening carried on, it seemed to be forgotten, and polite conversation resumed. At the end of the night, his parents spoke of how nice it was to meet her and how they hoped to see her again soon.

But Oscar did not forget.

He ruminated on it the whole way home, but decided to say nothing. It was gone. Done. Passed. And mentioning it would have done nothing but take away from the wonderful success of the evening – and that, for Oscar, was a huge achievement.

And he couldn't have asked for more – from April, or his parents.

15

Derek had never had a son.

Once, he had been engaged, a long time ago. It had ended when he chose to pursue a life of fighting the supernatural, and she saw it as a joke. He had never had a prolonged relationship since.

Was it something he regretted?

The relationship – maybe, maybe not. He'd had many valuable relationships, just none of them prolonged romantic encounters.

But a son, or a daughter. That was something he regretted. And possibly a void he fulfilled in those he mentored, but a void nonetheless.

As he looked at Charlie, colouring in with a spritely energy he would not be able to sustain, he wondered whether Charlie and his unborn child would have ever been alike. Given, he had never imagined having a child with a terminal illness, but if he had, he imagined his child would have dealt with it with the same tenacity and resolve that Charlie had.

"What's this?" Derek asked, stifling a groan as he leant

forward from his chair to see what the young lad was colouring in.

"It's The Hulk," Charlie answered. "He's the best superhero ever."

"The best, huh?"

"Yeah! He's green, and when he's angry he gets bigger and he smashes things."

"He smashes things?" Derek repeated with feigned amazement.

"Yeah!"

"But what about the people whose things he smashes? Does he at least pay the bill for it?"

"No. He doesn't pay bills. He's too cool for that."

Derek couldn't help but laugh. If only he'd have been too cool to pay bills. It would have made life so much simpler.

"So how are things, Charlie?"

"Okay," he responded, continuing to colour in his picture.

"And this creature you spoke of. Has he been back?"

Charlie's hand stopped colouring. His eyes stopped scanning the black outline before him and his limp body grew tense.

"Has he, Charlie?"

"I – I don't want to talk about that."

Charlie's hand started moving once more, but far slower, colouring with a distant wariness.

"Why not?"

"Because I don't want to. I want to talk about good things."

"But aren't you afraid he'll come back?"

"I said I don't want to talk about it. And it's a she."

Derek allowed a moment of contemplative silence to hang in the air, and Charlie's hand resumed speed, until he was colouring eagerly once more.

"Okay, I understand," Derek finally affirmed.

As he sat watching the boy, Derek noticed something glistening around his neck. Something that sparkled in the light.

"Charlie, what's this?" Derek asked, pointing at what he had just seen.

"This?" Charlie responded, lifting a pendant from under his hospital gown.

"Yes, what is it?"

"It's from my mum."

"Your mum?"

"Yes. She isn't with us anymore."

"I'm sorry to hear that."

"It's okay." He opened it, showing a picture of a beautiful brown-haired woman with bright-green eyes.

"Is that her?" Derek asked, taking the pendant in his hand and gazing upon it.

Charlie nodded.

"She's very pretty," Derek said.

"She was. I miss her a lot."

"I don't doubt you do."

Derek let the pendant go and sat back in his chair. Charlie tucked it back beneath his hospital gown and resumed his colouring.

Derek watched it hanging loosely, wondering what he would give the people he loved once he was gone.

16

Oscar managed to turn the key, open the front door, and nearly slip on a pile of unwanted bills without acknowledging it with any thought. He rubbed his eyes, wiping the tiredness off his face, but he could feel his eyelids drooping. Success or not, the evening with his parents had been stressful, and it had truly worn him down. Anxiety was tiresome, and he had been full of it in the hours leading up to dinner, and he was looking forward to bed.

"I'm going to get ready for bed," he told April as she closed the front door. "You coming?"

"Mmhm," she answered.

He threw his jacket over the sofa and stumbled through to the bedroom. He meandered into the bathroom, pouring water into the sink without switching the light on; any illumination would be likely to highlight those tired features on his face and expose them in the reflection of the mirror, and a bout of insecurity was not what he needed to go to sleep on. He rubbed a handful of soap over his face, washed it off, and rubbed the water from his skin with his Batman towel. For the next three minutes he brushed his teeth without acknowledging the back and forth movement of his toothbrush, doused with a small dollop of minty refreshment, courtesy of the nearby tube of Colgate. Once he was finished, he went to switch the light off, and ended up switching it on, forgetting that it had been off in the first place.

He switched it back off, rubbed his eyes, then dropped his jaw as he feasted his eyes on the sight of April standing before him, as naked as the day she was born.

"Apr–"

He couldn't even finish saying her name before she had flung herself toward him and thrusted her mouth so hard against his he winced in pain as he caught his bottom lip in his teeth.

Was this pregnancy hormones?

Hell, does it matter...

Oscar engaged, putting his hands on her back and stroking gently up her spine. Before he could move his hands any further she had grabbed his wrists and shoved them back behind his back. He went to put his arms back around her, but she forced them behind his back once more.

"Leave them," she instructed with deadly assertiveness, twisting her head from side to side as she pushed and pushed her lips against his.

Oscar opened his eyes momentarily, taken aback by her abrupt nature. This was nothing like he'd experienced before. Given, yes, his sexual experience was vastly inferior to hers; but in the many, many, many times they had entered foreplay in the last six months, there had never been hands restrained behind backs or kissing so hard it hurt.

She grabbed hold of his arms, squeezing against his limp biceps so hard he felt her thumbs rub against his bones. She threw him onto the bed.

As he bounced on the mattress, he looked up at her as if to say something – but what? What was he supposed to ask? It was strange, yes, but in that fleeting second he had before her harsh lips pounded back to his, his thoughts could not formulate the words to express his confusion, or how taken aback he was.

She didn't even undress him. He went to take his top off, but she just shoved his hands back against the mattress above his head and held them there with one single hand. She used the other to unleash his belt and push his trousers down just enough for her to be able to grab his stiff cock in her hand.

Within seconds she had mounted him, and he had entered her.

It hurt. Hurt in a way it never had before. It didn't feel warm or pleasurable like it normally did; it felt rough. Coarse. Unprepared.

He knew this was due to lack of foreplay. She wasn't wet enough, and this meant that his penis was rubbing against the dry surface of her insides. He felt his foreskin scrape up and down against the force of her movement. He went to object, but her hand covered his mouth before he could open it fully.

As he stared up at her he felt himself tremble. Her expression was different. There was something carnal about it. Her lip was aggressively curled, twisting into a sneer, and her nose ruffled up into a leering snarl. Her eyes were distant, yet piercingly close. A sinister glare, as if she was doing this because she hated him.

Her hand sunk from his mouth, down his chin, and to his throat. Her palm spread over his neck and squeezed, tightening and tightening until he couldn't breathe.

He tried to speak, but she tightened harder until he couldn't. He tried to choke, tried to clamber for air, but she refused to allow him the luxury of oxygen.

She moved faster. Riding harder and harder. Rubbing her rough insides against him to the point that he was now burning, like hot rubber wrapped around his genitals, static pushing against his skin.

He wanted to cry.

This didn't feel like sex.

Sex didn't always have to be intimate, sometimes it could be playful, or even rough – but this felt worse. Like an attack. An invasion of his rights. Forced upon him until his voice was stifled and he couldn't make enough sense of what was occurring to object.

She loosened her grip, pulled her hand back, and growled. A low-pitched, sinister growl.

"Apri–"

She sliced her hand across his cheek. A slap with her nails, as if instructing him to shut up. To dare not moan. To never say a word against what this dominant force chose to do.

She stopped.

Suddenly. Her movement stiffly, abruptly still. She remained in position, him inside of her, poised in limbo.

She dismounted.

Fell onto her side. Turned, lying away from him, curled up tightly into the foetal position.

In less than a minute her breathing was deep, and a gentle snore whispered out of her mouth.

Oscar couldn't make sense of what had just happened. He couldn't react. He couldn't speak.

It's not that he didn't appreciate the surprise element, nor that he expected every movement of their sex life to be gentle and passionate, just that he should be allowed to talk. To voice his objections, or guide her in what felt good. So often he had gone down on her and allowed her to guide him, in either a gentle, soothing voice, or with the gentle nudge of her hands against his head. An action he had welcomed, as it allowed him to ensure he was giving her as much pleasure as he could.

This was different.

This was… something else.

He hadn't even been able to talk to her enough to even withdraw his consent.

It was hostile. Forced. Aimed at the destruction of his self-worth. The abuse of an intimacy both he and she had rights to.

The events soared round his mind as he lay there, listening to the faint purr of her breathing.

17

An instant lurch awoke April from a deep, dreamless sleep. The light bursting between the lines of the blinds informed her it was morning, but she didn't have time to dwell on it as she ran to the bathroom.

She opened her mouth and vomit poured out of her. It burnt her neck, and left volatile lumps floating in her saliva. She spat, trying to get rid of the remnants, only to find herself violently heaving again, hurtling partly digested pieces into the toilet boil, with a small splatter decorating the toilet seat.

Morning sickness was a common trait of pregnancy, she knew that. But was it always meant to be this heavy? Even after she had drunk too much, her stomach would throw the contents of her stomach up her throat and out of her mouth in a way that left only a faint queasiness.

Yet, at that moment, she felt the need to fall onto her backside to avoid fainting. Blots of colours overtook her vision, masking the tiles of the bathroom with a hazy disguise.

Another gag jolted her body, along with another few gags, followed by a desperate sickness that made her sweat. She had already brought up most of the food in her stomach, meaning the final load had brought little more than blood.

She yearned for food to cure an eager hunger, but dared not eat. She had just emptied the contents of her belly and her body was requesting her to refill it, but she knew anything she put back in would just come up again.

She gagged once more. Except this time, she didn't feel the hot sensation of liquid and lumps pushing up her throat. It was something harder. Something small digging into her, giving a harsh, prickling sensation in her throat.

Another gag made it only intensify more. Her body convulsed a few times, and her mouth instinctively opened to allow the half-moon crescent shape of numerous nails to spew from her cracked lips.

She looked down at them with terror. They were thick enough to be toenails. They were yellow, as if they were infected, or long since dead.

Her eyes were transfixed.

Toenails?

She tried to justify it. Tried to convince herself that she had mistaken the sight, that they were something else. But there was such a large quantity of them that she was certain she wasn't mistaken.

There must have been a rational explanation, she was sure of it, but her manic thoughts could not clamber at one whatsoever.

Nails?

Had she swallowed them at some point that she didn't know?

She peered down at her bare feet. Her nails were short, as if recently cut – but she hadn't done that. At least, she had no recollection of it.

Was it something that you'd remember? Cutting your nails?

Or is it something you do without thinking, then forget

about, discarding the memory like the empty wrapper from a packet of food?

Except, how would they end up in her digestive system?

She had little time to dwell on it before her body fought against her once more. She gagged. Her body convulsed even harsher, even her arms and legs forced to twitch with the upward writhing of her chest. She coughed and spluttered as she felt something else push through, carving against the inside of her neck as if it were a knife marking a stone wall.

It was big. Thick. Coarse.

It grated against the inside of her throat. Against the passage she would use to swallow food, a passage that only seemed to be growing narrower and narrower.

It was long. Something rough, long, and...

The top of it came to her mouth. She could feel a tuft against her tongue, like numerous strings wrapped into a coil, brushing against her gums.

She reached her hand behind her teeth and grabbed hold of it. It was frayed. Harsh. Grating against her hand.

Another retch forced it further upwards and she managed to pull the end of it out of her mouth.

Rope.

She convulsed in an action somewhere between a choke and a gag. She could still feel it stuck, tightly wedged, blocking her breath. Bumpy, coarse, hurting her, frightening her.

She pulled it out further, reeling it through her mouth.

A small, yet thick, rough rope. Burnt at the edges, bristly along its edge.

The abrasive surface pushed itself further upwards with another gag.

Then her need to be sick stopped.

Her whole body tensed. She was no longer gagging, but it was still stuck, still lodged in her throat.

So she pulled.

She grabbed the edges between her fingers and yanked it out. In a sudden movement at first then, upon feeling its discomfort harden, a smoother, gradual pull.

It extracted, inch by inch, until the full length was out, at least the length of two long rulers. It was followed by a mouthful of blood that she spat into the toilet, but hit the floor as dizziness took over her aim. But she didn't care. A few drops of blood on the floor was the least of her worries.

Rope.

From her stomach.

How?

How had it–

She gagged once more, and her whole body convulsed into a violent jolt that sent her hurtling forward and sent her head smacking onto the side of the toilet.

As her skull combined with the porcelain of the toilet rim, a crucifix punched itself against the toilet bowl.

At least, that's what she thought it was.

Because that's the last thing she saw before she blacked out.

When she came around, she was still alone in the bathroom. Oscar was still enjoying a leisurely lie-in in the bedroom behind the en suite, completely unaware of the terror she was experiencing.

She peered into the toilet bowl, checking that she hadn't imagined it, checking that she had actually vomited those things.

But all she found as she moved her prying eyes was a clean bowl, and a complete absence of objects.

She stared, wondering whether she had really experienced it or if it had all been a dream.

She was tempted to believe the latter.

But the rough feeling of the inside of her throat, as if the rough edge of a rope had been dragged through it, made the nagging voice at the back of her mind believe otherwise.

(5 MONTHS)

18

A LOT OF TALKING TOOK PLACE. A LOT OF HYPOTHESISING, debating, and skirting around possible solutions without any firm decision – as most conversations intended to be decisive generally go.

Derek didn't care for a bit of it.

The whole time Jason and Julian stood debating the merits of extra security at the hospital, about how much to tell whom about the demonic aspect and what role Julian would play in all this. Derek sat still, staring across the children's ward and the ill young child stuck in the middle of all this nonsensical debating.

Charlie.

A bright young boy, aged ten.

Desperately unlucky.

He didn't deserve it. Derek was aware it would be unlikely you would ever attribute someone of being deserving of such an illness, but such a thought was ever more pertinent with this child. The lad had a zest for life, an enthusiasm in the mundane, and an infectious curiosity that had gripped Derek.

With the busyness of Julian's chaotic attempts to make sense of what does not make sense, he seemed to be missing out on that. That there was a child at the centre of this – no, that there were *children* at the centre of this – all of them longing for their opportunity at life. An opportunity nature had given them, then snapped it away like dangling thread before a helpless kitten.

"Do you know how much I've had to do to secure this?" Jason was saying. "With the budget the station's got, and with the way they look at me when I mention these damn cases, I never thought in a million years I'd actually manage to arrange for a permanent police presence here."

"It's not that," Julian responded, shaking his head.

"One officer. Stationed here, on rotation."

"It's useless."

"How, exactly?"

Julian sighed. He cupped his hands over his face. Derek could see how tired he was, you only had to look at his drooping eyes to see what the stress of this case was doing. But that was Julian – not someone to let a case go without doing everything he could to help the people involved, even if his ideas were irrefutably stubborn.

At least that was one strong trait that persisted in Julian. An unrelenting commitment to the cause.

"Just – what are you going to tell them?" retorted Julian. "That they need to look out for a demon? No, it's not going to work. If anything, we want to catch this thing – if we don't, we won't stand a chance."

"So we use a bunch of sick kids as bait?"

"That's not what I'm saying!"

"Then what is it you're saying?"

"I'm saying that a human police presence will not help, and if anything, will hinder. We want to see this beast found, don't we? We want to exorcise it from this ward? Well, we need it to show up again to do that."

"Oh right. I see. I'll just go make a phone call and say the children's ward with a potential ghostly serial killer doesn't need the extra protection I worked my arse off to get."

"No, Jason, you're not listening."

Derek's head dropped into his hands.

Their voices faded to a distant whine, like a muffle through headphones. His energy left him in a sudden spurt of pain, like some kind of vacuum had come along and sucked every piece of his liveliness out of him.

Charlie seemed so far away now.

The room stretched, pushing away from Derek, pulling further from his reach.

He tried reaching his hand out. Tried pushing his arm out and grasping it, but his arm didn't move. It just didn't move.

Charlie.

Colouring in.

Dropped his pen.

"You've dropped–" Derek attempted to say, but found his words coming out as a low wheeze, an old man's cough that stung his throat.

Charlie couldn't reach them.

The pen was on the floor. Charlie was too high up. The boy was leaning over, but he couldn't reach it. And he was too weak to get off the bed.

Derek reached out once more.

His chest stopped rising.

His arm held rigid, then slid downwards, falling down the spinning tunnel before him. Charlie turned to a blur, as did the floor, the luminescence of the lights, the faded corridor, the ceiling, the... the... the...

Derek fell.

Reaching his hand out for the pen, he toppled over and pounded on the floor.

The abrupt commotion that ensued around him turned to circles spinning over his mind.

He wasn't breathing.

He was sure he wasn't breathing.

Someone was by him. He could hear them talking, could feel their soft hands on his chest, but they weren't there.

They were, and they weren't.

He was pushed onto his back.

A haze of blurs.

Pumping.

His chest, pumping.

Lunging upwards. Lunging downwards.

No breathing.

Still no breathing.

Still no.

Still.

THEN

19

ANOTHER DAY, ANOTHER ANSWER PHONE MESSAGE.

Martin was struggling enough without having to hear that voice again.

The same well-spoken, articulate, ever-calm voice.

"Martin, I know you've been ignoring my calls, but please, I implore you to respond."

He seethed over Derek's words. *I implore you to respond.* Who talks like that? That was the thing about Derek's evident education – it had always shown Martin what a difference in backgrounds they had.

And why was he ringing on a landline? Martin had a mobile. No one ever used landlines before. Derek was so stubborn.

Martin shook his head. Ran his hands over his face.

None of this had ever mattered before. He was looking for things to hate, and he knew it.

What did it matter if Derek didn't phone Martin's mobile? What's more, Martin had always found Derek to be accepting of anyone, of any background, so long as their intentions were noble. In fact, he'd...

Stop it.

Martin willed himself to hate his former mentor. To despise the man that he was.

The phone rang again.

"For fuck's sake," he muttered.

In a moment of sudden decision, he swung the phone from the wall and to his ear.

"What?" he barked.

"Martin?" came Derek's distressed voice. "Oh, I am so glad you picked up. Did you know it was me?"

"Of course I knew, no one else rings a landline."

"Oh. Well, I guess I'm still behind the times in some way. How are you?"

Martin huffed. How was he? After all this time, Derek had the nerve to phone him up and ask how he was.

"Derek, I don't want to speak to you, man," Martin said. "I told you."

"Yes, I know that. And if that is what you wish, then I will respect your wish, although it is against my own. I just thought I'd have one last try. As, well, I may not be able to for a while."

"Why?"

"Well, you see, I have myself in a little bit of a pickle. A girl called Anna, she died, and I… well, I needn't bore you with the details. I'm going away, and let's just say you wouldn't be able to find me. So I thought it best to find you. One last time, if that's what it is."

Martin looked out of his window. A young boy held his father's hand as they walked toward the park. Once there, the boy smiled at his father, running to the swing set. The father watched on with a smile that only a proud father would wear.

A father. Martin had never known what it was like to have such a thing.

Then again, he could have known what it was like to be a father. If Derek hadn't messed up. If Derek hadn't…

"Well, you found me," Martin observed after a few lengthy moments of silence.

"And? Would you permit me to meet with you? Perhaps introduce you to a few people who may be able to help you with–"

"I don't want anything from you."

A cold silence followed.

"I understand, Martin. Just know I had the best of intentions."

Martin laughed mockingly.

"Fuck you, Derek. Fuck you to hell. The best of intentions? You let that woman, and the child, die. You let them fucking die, you arsehole."

"I did not let them–"

"Yes you did!" Martin willed himself to calm down. He was breathing fast, pacing the room with an aimless rapidity. "Yes, you did."

"I promise you, Martin, I never intended–"

"Is that it?" Martin felt tears accumulating in the corners of his eyes, but he willed them away. He was not about to give Derek that.

Talking to Derek meant having to face up to what happened to Madelina. To his child.

It was easier to be angry.

It had always been easier to be angry.

"Yes," Derek said resolutely. "I guess it is."

"Bye then. Don't call again."

Martin punched the handset against the receiver.

He waited a few moments, then ripped the receiver off the wall, tearing the wires apart.

Now there was no way Derek could contact him.

He punched the wall.

His fist hurt, but not enough.

He punched it again.

This was all Derek's fault.

Madelina. His child. All of it. Everything. It was Derek's fault that Martin felt like this. That he felt like he didn't want to live. Like death would be the best answer.

He had no one. Nothing.

He used to have Derek. He was going to have Madelina. And a child.

Now he was alone, again. Alone as he had always been. No mother or father to take him in. No friends to open their arms.

No mentor to comfort him.

Alone.

Again.

Angry. Bitter. Fuming.

It was Derek's fault.

All of it. Everything.

He bowed his head.

It was Derek's fault.

If he kept telling himself that, he almost believed it.

NOW

20

An overhead light pushed its beams upon the plain room.

A steady beeping sifted into Derek's mind.

As his eyes gradually opened, the beeping continued. Until it made sense. Until he saw where he was.

A hospital gown. A bed. Sterile, cold, pale walls.

No.

This was not where he wanted to be.

He tried to lift himself, but his body was too heavy. He could barely lift a hand, never mind prop his torso up.

But this wasn't where he was meant to be.

It wasn't…

"It's okay," came a familiar voice. "You're alive, if that's what you're wondering."

With a great deal of energy that probably looked like nothing to a bystander, Derek flopped his head to the side and cast his heavy eyes on the concerned face of Julian.

"I said I didn't want to come here," Derek barked.

Well, attempted to bark.

His disdain wasn't as clear as he intended, such was the slow, struggling nature of the words he spoke.

"Well that's probably why you've ended up here," Julian said. "Because you refused to in the first place. Then look at what happened."

Derek didn't try to lift his head again. It was too much effort. Instead, he twitched his eyes back and forth.

He was in the ward adjacent to the children's ward. The cancer ward. He could see the children's ward through the window of the door.

"Why am I here?" he asked.

"You stopped breathing," Julian answered. "They had to perform CPR."

"Why did I stop breathing?"

"Why?" Julian's hands gripped the arms of his seat, and Derek could see it was all he could do to contain his fury. "Because you have cancer, Derek. Why won't you understand that?"

"I do understand that–"

"Clearly not! You almost–"

Julian looked away. He couldn't say it.

"Almost what?" Derek prompted. He wanted to hear it.

"Almost died," Julian replied. "You almost died, Derek."

"But I am going to die, Julian. And probably very soon."

"So that's it? You give up like that?"

Derek's lips managed to curl into a weak smile.

"I'm older than most people who survive this," Derek admitted. "I've made my peace with it."

Julian glared back at Derek. For a while they just sat there, an intense silence piercing the tension, so much firing around their heads.

"Well maybe you have," Julian said, full of venom. "But that doesn't mean everyone else has."

Julian stood up with full intention to storm out, but hovered in the doorway. He placed his hands firmly on his hips, dropping his gaze to the floor.

He looked over his shoulder at the weak man staring back.

"The nurses said to get some rest. Or you won't be getting out of bed."

Julian left.

But a shadow remained.

Derek frowned.

A shadow hovered. Lingering in the doorway. The shadow's head rotated, twisting toward him.

Derek peered into the doorway. Tried to see it. Tried to make it out.

But his eyes.

They were so heavy.

A face appeared on the shadow. A contorted, falsely feminine, narrow-eyed visage of abhorrence.

Its mouth opened.

Was this what they had seen? The children? Could he see it now he was so close to death?

His mind did not give him the luxury of dwelling on his thoughts. Thoughts often are unreliable and bizarre when in the place between sleeping and awake. And those thoughts drifted away into the submerged subconscious of his thoughts.

Yet, as he drifted back to sleep, he was sure he could hear, ever so gently, a low cackling.

(4 MONTHS)

21

MOTHERCARE WASN'T A SHOP OSCAR HAD BEEN TO BEFORE – THE most obvious reason being that he hadn't ever expected a baby before, but also because he had found it a little scary. He was unsure why – it was hardly a place to dread, it was just full of children's stuff. It could have been that it made it real; not the lovely child on the way, but the huge burden that child was going to place on his finances. The stuff in here hadn't particularly received huge praise for its affordable pricing.

But, as soon as he crossed the threshold, he was taken aback by a delicate aroma of talcum powder that sent him back to his childhood. Nothing was crowded together; the items that helped with babies in all varieties of circumstances were arranged with aisles large enough to fit two prams down. The lighting was bright, but not too bright, with a slight orange-and-blue tint. It made him feel light, and gave him flutters of excitement for what was to come.

April, reluctantly attached to him via the sweaty palm clamped around his, looked less than impressed. He didn't take this personally. She looked immensely tired, as if she had been dragged through hell backwards. Her skin had come out with dark, splotchy patches, in the form of large, dark circles placed sporadically across her face and her arms. Her eyes looked weary, with barely a white space across her retina void of bloodshot veins.

Most grotesque of all – though Oscar would never verbalise such a description aloud – were her gums. They had dried up and bled, until the spaces around her teeth were prickling with flakes of dried skin.

"Hey," Oscar offered, doing his best to comfort her with a hand running down her hair. "You okay?"

"Fine," she answered in a low, raspy voice.

"I've got the list. If you want to sit down then honestly, it wouldn't matter."

"I don't want to sit down," she grumbled blankly. Her eyes did not rise to his, instead directing what small part of her pupil Oscar could glimpse from beneath her drooping eyelids at the ground. She looked absent of consciousness, like she was a zombie working on automatic. Honestly, if she sat down and remained really still, you would be excused for wondering if she was dead.

"Well, hey, we need prams first, and they are over here," Oscar said, trying to lighten the mood. He directed her to a few larger shelves that displayed some of the prams.

He had never realised there would be so many varieties and colours of one simple object as a pram.

Leaning forward, he took the price tag of the nearest item and turned it so that it was visible. He recoiled, and decided it was best not to show it to April, as it may just push her over the edge.

"Well, hey, maybe we'll go second hand," Oscar suggested. "Or look at a really small one. Like these over here."

He led her, dragging her like she was a pack of weights, toward a few of the smaller prams that appeared to be more toward their price range.

"What do you think of these, April?" he asked.

No reply.

"April?"

Nothing.

"Hey, April, what do you think?"

He turned to April, but she was not looking in his direction. Her eyes had opened wide, far wider than he had seen them in weeks, and her empty pupils were fixed on something. Something across the store.

He peered in the direction she was staring, trying to find what it was. There was no particular item that stuck out, nothing that took his attention.

Then he saw what she was staring at. Because he was staring right back.

It was a toddler. Barely able to walk. Rooted to the spot.

His mum was trying with all her might to drag the child away, but the child was immovable. Gravity seemed to be weighing him down with an irregular certainty, an anomaly of the human condition. For his mother dragged, and dragged, and dragged, but had to stop for fear of accidentally pulling the boy's underdeveloped arm from its loose socket.

"April?"

Nothing.

Her eyes were transfixed. The gaze between them was fixed with such rigidity, such stubbornness, that it seemed impossible to break. It was like an invisible laser had fired between their eye sockets and would not shift.

"April, come on."

Oscar waved a hand in front of her eyes.

No movement. No reaction. Her body was as stiff and as heavy as a box of wood.

She was not blinking.

Come to think of it, Oscar was sure he hadn't seen her blink for at least a minute.

"April, you're freaking me out," he tried, hoping he could reason with her. But his voice was like rain falling on brick. It did no damage, made no difference, and just glided off into a puddle on the floor.

"April, please, would you just–"

Oscar's voice shrivelled up, caught in his throat. He stared at the floor, mortified as he processed the sight beneath him.

He looked away, then looked back again, as if he had to convince himself it was real.

A steady stream of blood glided down the inside of her leg, and seeped from beneath her dress. It ran down her bare ankles, over her socks, and landed in a steady pool beside her Converses.

"April, we need to go."

Nothing.

"April, you're bleeding."

Not a flutter of the eyelids. Not a difference to the stone eyes that did not break or falter.

"April, we don't know what this is; we need to get to a doctor."

Her lips pursed. The first movement she had made whilst her and the child had been in this bizarre transfixion.

"April, are you–"

April muttered something.

"What?"

She muttered something again.

"What is it?"

Then, with an uncomfortable seething quality, a low-pitch intensity, with drawn-out syllables and vehement snarls, she spoke a few slow, specific words at the child:

"I. Am going. To fucking *kill* you."

Her eyelids closed, her body loose, and she fell to the floor. Oscar just about managed to catch her before she hit the ground.

He shook her, trying to wake her.

The boy she had stared at was gone. Finally relinquished his fixed stare and allowed his mother to drag him away.

Oscar shook April, terrified, petrified as to what may have happened to her, and the baby.

"Help!" he shouted.

He shook her again.

"Help! Please, somebody help!"

A crowd gathered, and from that crowd someone offered help, but Oscar couldn't hear them. It all turned to a distant buzzing.

All he could focus on was the love of his life, bleeding on the floor of Mothercare.

22

OSCAR'S NAILS HAD BEEN BITTEN ON AND CHEWED MORE IN TEN minutes than they had in his entire life.

He sat on the edge of the chair, eagerly awaiting the verdict, desperate to hear what the doctor had to say.

April lay back on the bed. Unresponsive. In a diluted vegetative state.

Her eyes were open, but beneath them was nothing. The spritely, friendly smile and sparkling eyes that she once had – her loving, doting smiles – were gone, replaced by coldness. By absence of life. By something taking over her that he could not quite understand.

The doctor finally returned to the room and sat opposite them. She gave her a calm smile, and allowed it to spread from bouncy cheek to bouncy cheek. It gave a small amount of reassurance to Oscar, which was quickly replaced by a reminder of why he was there.

"The baby is fine," she told him. "It's there, its heart is beating; there is nothing wrong."

"They why – why was she bleeding?"

"I know it's alarming, and you absolutely did the right thing by making the emergency appointment – but you don't need to worry. Sometimes these things can happen. They aren't common, but they are still normal."

"Bleeding is normal? Doctor, it was dripping down her leg."

"Well, yes, bleeding can be a sign of something very wrong. But we have looked, and looked, and she is okay. We've checked for signs of vaginal infections, placental abruptions, vasa praevia – everything we can think of. Nothing."

Oscar looked back at the doctor, unconvinced.

"I know it's unsettling, but we have checked everything, and the baby is fine. April is fine. It may just be due to cervical changes."

Oscar turned to April. Watched her vacant eyes stare across the room. Not moving. Not twitching. Her arms didn't move to fidget, her legs didn't move to gain more comfort. The only movement she made was the lethargic rising of her chest as she slowly breathed.

"You say she's fine, but – just look at her."

The doctor turned to look at April. She took a moment to take her appearance in, to allow herself to study April's absent eyes and pale skin. She sighed, deciding on what words she was to use.

"Doctor? Do you really think this is normal?"

The doctor turned her gaze toward Oscar.

"It's understandable."

"What?"

"Pregnancy is a stressful experience, and a difficult one. April is obviously tired, and obviously finding it difficult."

"Doctor, she's not even aware we're talking about her."

In a swift, unprecedented motion, April's head turned to face Oscar. Her eyes met his, and he saw nothing of her brightness casting a light over him.

"I'm fine," April stated.

"Is that all you can say?" Oscar replied.

"Don't talk about me like I'm not in the room."

"I'm not, I'm not," Oscar insisted, leaning forward and placing a hand on her leg. He was taken aback by how cold her skin was; it was more like he was placing his hand on an ice pack than on the leg of the loving mother of his child.

"I just need you to get off my back."

"I'm not on your back, April, I'm doing all I can to help you."

"Look," the doctor interjected, "this is a difficult time. For both of you. Why not just go home, go to bed, and have a relaxing weekend?"

Oscar sighed.

The doctor didn't know.

She didn't live with this. She didn't stare at this catatonic state every day. It was like this child had consumed her. It was like tiredness had taken over her body, and all that was left was a depraved, distant woman who used to be in love with him.

"Whatever happens," the doctor directed at Oscar, "you need positive energy."

"Positive energy?"

"Yes. And I'm afraid to say, it needs to come from you, Oscar. April will be difficult. Sorry if that offends you, darling" – April didn't react – "but she will be. And you just need to prepare for that."

"Prepare for it? How? What am I meant to do?"

"Get her a hot water bottle. Play soothing music. Promise her you'll do whatever it takes. Oscar, I've seen many pregnant women, and I promise you – you will be fine."

Oscar looked to April. He didn't feel like it would be fine.

But like she said, she'd seen many pregnant women.

He hadn't.

Maybe this was normal.

"After all," the doctor added, "you don't want to be stressed for when she comes along."

Oscar's head swung toward the doctors. His expression changed, overcome with joy and amazement.

"She?" he asked. "Did you say she? I mean, you were able to see this time?"

The doctor grinned.

"Yes, Oscar. You are having a daughter."

(3 MONTHS)

23

IF DEREK FELT OPTIMISTIC ABOUT ESCAPING THE HOSPITAL, THOSE hopes diminished as soon as he stepped out of bed.

He'd imagined leaping out the window via a rope, dropping down to the floor, and running until he legs would not carry him anymore.

Or even sneaking down the corridor, perhaps disguising himself in a doctor's uniform, and finding a car conveniently parked with the keys haphazardly left stuck in the ignition.

Maybe he could re-enact *The Great Escape. The Shawshank Redemption.* Have an iconic soundtrack accompany his rapid progress as he dug a hole and appeared at the exact location he wished to be.

But, after making the decision to get a paper cup of water from the fountain outside his room, he had endured the struggle it took to get from his bed to his feet, to hobble across the wall to the door, having to lean his hands against the bumpy paint job of the sickeningly pale room, then reach the doorway, out of breath – it only highlighted to him how weak he was, and how much he depended on the help of the people in this building.

He used to be able feel the life dripping out of him by the day. Now, he felt it going by the hour. The more he tried to regain strength, the more he sweated, the more he struggled. Every movement seemed to take the effort of a marathon. His breathing quickened pace, his blood pumped, his sweat dripped down his forehead – all from walking across the room.

As he paused in the doorway, staring at the water fountain a few metres away, the target, the mission, he leant against the door frame.

It seemed so easy.

Just a few steps away.

Just a few steps.

Just a few.

Just nothing.

There was no *just* anymore. It was all an effort. All a drag.

If felt like death was waiting for him just past that water fountain. Hanging around, chilling out, hovering somewhere it could not be seen by Derek, but always had its beady eyes watching. Waiting.

Tasting the inevitable.

"Derek!" came the concerned voice of Julian, rushing down the corridor toward him. "What are you doing?"

"Water," Derek said between breaths.

"Here, let me," Julian insisted, helping Derek to a nearby seat.

Once Julian made sure Derek was sat comfortably, and wasn't going to slip off the chair, he strolled to the water fountain with a sickening ease, poured a paper cone, and handed it to Derek. Derek took it in his shaking hand, trying to steady his arms enough so he didn't splash the water over his lap. He brought it to his lips and felt the water cascade down his dry throat.

He was aware of Julian staring.

"What?" Derek grunted.

"Nothing," said Julian.

"I know what I look like. I know how I am. You don't need to look so concerned."

"You know that's not what it is."

"Then what is it?"

"It's just what's happened today, you know. It's tough."

Derek grew confused.

"What do you mean, what's happened?"

Julian's expression turned to that of perplexity, looking quizzically at Derek.

"You don't know?" Julian asked.

"Don't know what?" Derek knew he sounded impatient, but he couldn't help it.

"Oh. Well, I suppose you wouldn't have known. I guess we've been so busy dealing with it we didn't tell you."

"Busy dealing with *what*, Julian?"

Julian hesitated.

"Another child died. Was killed. It looked like it was whatever this thing is again."

Derek was stumped. Confused. It took longer than it would have done if he was healthy to comprehend what was said.

"Which child?"

"Oh, I can't remember the kid's name."

Jason's head appeared from the children's ward a few doors down the corridor.

"Julian, you need to come look at this," Jason called.

"I'll be right back," Julian told Derek, and rushed to the nearby door, disappearing behind it.

A child.

Died.

Another one.

Same demon.

Then it hit him like an elbow in the throat.

What about Charlie? Was it him? It couldn't be. It couldn't.

There were so many children on that ward, it was statistically improbable.

Still, Derek knew he wouldn't calm down until he found out for sure.

He used the chair to push himself to his feet. His legs buckled like two twigs trying to hold up a box of bricks, but he steadied them; with all the will he had, he steadied them.

Resting his hands on the wall, he pushed himself, dragged himself, pulled himself across the corridor.

The door was so close, but it felt like it was in the next building.

His breathing quickened pace. He wasn't sure whether it was his anxiety or his depleting energy levels, but he forced himself to ignore it, forced himself to keep struggling forward.

His hands clenched the door frame. The painting of a child on the nearest inside wall did not give him the reassuring sense of childish optimism he was sure was intended. In fact, the pictures of clowns and the scribbles and drawings hung up, decorations supplied by sick children come and gone, did nothing but push his fear upwards through his chest until it came pouring out of his throat in a quivering mumble.

Twisting around the door, he paused, looking back and forth.

Getting his bearings.

Adjusting his vision.

But he already knew the truth.

The sad thing about finding the certainty that truth brings is that denial is no longer an option. One has no choice but to be honest about what faces them.

And what faced Derek was police tape around the space that Charlie had once occupied.

Curtains were drawn, but they did nothing to disguise the blood splashed against the inside. It pushed through, glaringly visible, multiple streaks of obvious red.

As he fell to his knees he felt his kneecaps pound, the bone punching against the solid floor.

He did not care.

Nor did he care about the multitude of doctors and nurses rushing to his side, dragging him to his knees. He'd have tried to object, to scream or kick, if he had the ability. But he didn't.

Because Charlie was dead.

Charlie. Was dead.

And he hadn't been well enough to save him.

24

Oscar's eyes sprung open like a hook had found its way under his eyelids and yanked them open. His eyeballs felt like they had outgrown his eye sockets. As he shifted his vision from side to side they felt swollen, like they had been ripped out and placed back again.

Darkness.

Bed.

April.

She was next to him, curled up into a ball, facing the outside of the bed. Calm.

Her belly was bigger. With his child inside. His daughter.

It was an incredible thought.

A human life lived inside of her. A person, soon to be born, soon to be loved. He was already bursting with affection for this girl, ready to take care of her, provide for her, and give her the love he never truly felt from his parents.

Not that they were bad parents, quite the opposite – they took care of him, provided him with pocket money, gave him a safe home. They never physically hurt him in any way.

But their love, their affection, it had always felt conditional.

Like he would only get it if he fulfilled their expectations. If he got straight A's, went to university, went to extra-curricular sports clubs – none of which he ever actually did.

But now, as he turned and leant his arm over the woman he loved, the woman he had only dreamt of meeting and being with, he placed his hand on her belly. Softly brushing the safe home where his child was being kept.

An abrupt whisper came out of April's mouth, and he retracted his hand quickly.

"April?" Oscar said softly.

Nothing. She was asleep.

He placed his hand on her belly once more, and the whisper started again.

She was saying something. There were words, he just couldn't make them out.

He leant closer. Took his hand away.

Listened.

Nothing. Then he placed his hand back again, and she whispered once more.

As soon as he managed to make out a few syllables, he realised it wasn't English. It sounded different. Old.

Latin.

He'd heard enough Latin incantations within his work to recognise it. But he didn't understand it.

He listened carefully once more, but she said nothing.

He placed his hand on her belly.

Her lips pursed once more, and the whisper came out.

Was this only happening when he touched his baby?

He listened. Took in the words she was saying, trying to make out the sound.

"Filia mea. Filia mea. Filia mea."

As he leant closer, his hand pressed more firmly against her belly, the whispering grew more aggressive.

"Filia mea. Filia mea erit tuae mortis."

Oscar leapt out of bed, put on a hoodie, and quietly left the bedroom. He entered the living room and made his way to the bookshelf, looking for the book he was after.

A Latin-to-English dictionary.

He found it and placed it on the table.

He flicked through the F's, found the word *filia,* and scribbled its meaning on a nearby piece of paper.

Daughter.

He flicked through to the M's and found *mea.*

My.

"Daughter? My?" he muttered, then realised the words needed to be switched around. "My daughter."

How strange.

My daughter? What a weird thing to be whispering.

He sifted through the pages to *Erit.*

Will be.

To *tuae.*

Your.

He paused. He was pretty sure he knew what *mortis* meant. It was too close to mortician.

He reluctantly turned the pages, finding the right one, and stared at it with a mind full of perplexity.

It was… strange. To say the least.

Death.

Will be your death.

Finally, the words she was muttering, bizarrely whispering to herself, oddly mumbling with no awareness, in a language she couldn't possibly be fluent in, sunk into place.

Oscar's mouth moved to the syllables, but they didn't sound.

He shook his head.

There had to be a rational explanation.

Finally, his mind took control. His mouth formed the

words, and he repeated her words in English as a reflection of what she was saying.

"My daughter. My daughter. My daughter."

He ran his hand through his sweaty hair.

"My daughter will be your death."

His thoughts struggled for a rational, coherent understanding, to form words that could make sense of it, to create a feeling of comprehension.

They came out with nothing.

It was then that he realised what he could no longer deny.

He needed help.

(2 MONTHS)

25

Derek's eyes opened faintly from his afternoon nap to see Oscar sat quietly at his bedside.

"Hey," Oscar greeted him, placing a cup of tea on the table next to Derek. "I got this for you."

"Thanks," Derek acknowledged.

Derek tried sitting up, and in his struggle, Oscar stood up and lifted Derek's pillows, helping him into a sitting position.

"That okay?" Oscar checked.

"Great, thanks."

"Would you like your tea?"

"Yes, please."

Oscar passed Derek his cup of tea, placing it into both hands. Derek lifted it to his mouth and let it sink down his parched throat, relishing the warmth and reassurance that a cup of tea always brings.

"Thank you."

"You're welcome."

"So what are you doing here?" Derek mused. "Haven't you got a pregnant girlfriend to take care of?"

"Yes, but I thought I'd take half an hour off to come and see you. Check you are okay. You also need help, after all."

"Well, I appreciate your company, Oscar, but I assure you I don't need help."

Derek realised how silly the words were as soon as they left him. He hadn't even been able to sit up and have a cup of tea without the generosity of Oscar. But, like a polite young man, Oscar allowed the comment to settle without objecting, allowing Derek his pride.

"So how are things taking care of a pregnant woman?"

Oscar blew an overinflated sigh out of his mouth to signal his answer to the question.

"That tough, huh?"

"This pregnancy, it's... Well, it's had its complications."

"They all do."

"Yes, but I imagine this one is particularly difficult."

"And how are you managing it? Are you taking care of yourself?"

Oscar shifted uncomfortably in his seat. He looked like he wanted to give an affirmative answer, but struggled to do so.

"I just keep thinking, you know. What if this child ends up with as much complications as the pregnancy?"

"And what if it does?"

"It'll be tough."

"Would you stick by her?"

Oscar feigned confusion.

"Are you kidding?"

"You two do seem to really get on."

"Man, we do, we just – it's great, you know?"

Derek laughed.

"No, I don't," he said. "I'm afraid I had my heart broken long ago."

"I'm sorry."

"Tell me about it, then. The way you feel. I'm curious what

earth-shattering love is like."

Oscar smiled and bowed his head for a moment, collecting his thoughts. As his head rose again, he seemed to have gained a new sense of vigour and enthusiasm.

"Like there's no one in the world but us."

"But this child wasn't planned," Derek said honestly. "How are you going to cope?"

"With great energy and enthusiasm, my friend," Oscar asserted with a large grin. "When I'm with April, it's like – I'm not just a better person, but the truest person I am. Like, everything changes."

Derek felt a sharp sting of happiness, in recognition of the evident happiness Oscar undoubtedly felt.

"The world just sinks away," Oscar continued. "And it's just me and her. Us against the world. And now it's going to be three. And, I – I can't wait."

"What if the baby–"

"I don't care. I know what you're about to say, and whatever the baby brings, I will do whatever to protect that child, and to protect April."

As Derek's eyes met Oscar's, he could see that he meant it.

"She changed my life. And I can never repay that."

His phone beeped. He glanced at it.

"I'm needed in the other room. Are you going to be okay?"

"I'll be perfect."

"See you in a bit," Oscar said with a warm smile, and left.

Derek watched him leave, thinking about him. Thinking about the excellent young man he was turning into. Thinking about how April could not have found a more perfect partner to support him.

Regretting that he would likely not live long enough to see him grow into an amazing Sensitive.

In that moment, Derek decided that Oscar was truly remarkable.

26

"IF YOU'RE SURE YOU'RE UP FOR THIS, APRIL," JULIAN REPEATED for the who-knows-what time, "and only if."

"I'm not a piece of glass that's going to shatter and break," April insisted. "I can still work."

Oscar wasn't so sure.

April was an independent person with a sturdy head upon her shoulders, and he did not doubt that she knew her own limits. It wasn't up to him to insist that she does or doesn't work, but he was worried. Especially with the complications of the pregnancy; the bleeding, the mumbling in her sleep, the staring at random children.

Not to mention how big she was. It was less than eight weeks until the due date, and she was having to push herself off every chair, lean over as she walked. To him, she looked stunning. But to Julian, she must look sweaty, uncomfortable, and downright short-tempered.

"Well, if you're sure," Julian went on. "We could really do with someone, just to tell us what we're dealing with here."

"I'll do my best."

The nurses and doctors hadn't taken as much convincing as

Julian thought they would. Jason hadn't had to explain the situation for long until they were setting up an area for them to work, and standing aside as they took over the children's ward.

Thing is, that shouldn't be so surprising. The doctors would know the cause of death; they would be able to see that it wasn't natural.

And anyone who spent more than a minute in that room would be able to feel the sickening cold that chilled everyone's bones. There was something there, and it was evil, no doubt about it. You didn't have to be a Sensitive to see that.

April stepped forward. She closed her eyes and bowed her head.

Julian nodded at a nearby nurse, who turned off the lights in response.

Doctors, nurses, police, patients – everyone in the vicinity stopped what they were doing and watched. Whether out of helpless dread, optimistic hope, or just sheer, unadulterated curiosity, all eyes were on her. The only sound was the beeping of the life machines. The only thoughts were of the unknown, of what was going to happen next.

Everyone's thoughts, that was, but Oscar's.

He wasn't as keen to put April in striking distance of whatever entity was at work in her state. She was heavily pregnant, and heavily stressed. But he remembered what she had told him the previous night.

"I have to work, Oscar. I have to. It could be the only thing stopping me going completely crazy."

Oscar was hurt, though he knew it was unfair. He had hoped to be the only thing stopping her from going completely crazy. Though, if anything, he felt like a hindrance. Nothing he did, however caring or with the best of intentions, seemed to make the slightest bit of difference.

He felt useless.

Worse than useless.

"I can do this, trust me," she had said. "I would not do anything if I thought there was a single chance it would hurt our daughter. But, fact is, children are dying. And I can help."

She was right.

Of course, she was. She always was. So much so, it was infuriating. But that was part of why he loved her.

And boy, did he love her.

Not just because he was infatuated. At first, maybe, yes. But it had become so much more than that, so much more than her being the only cool girl looking in his direction. His caring for her ran deep; it was in his blood, in his mind, in every thought. It affected every action. Everything he did, he wondered how he would tell her about it later. He thought about what their future could be like.

She was everything.

Julian lit three candles that formed a triangle around April.

"Okay," he softly spoke. "When you're ready."

April descended to her knees. She closed her eyes, lifted her arms, and remained motionless.

She waited.

Breathing.

Oscar watched her. Getting a feeling, deep inside of him, that this was wrong. This was all wrong.

"The entity in this ward," April spoke. "The entity within. I speak to you."

Every eye was on her. Poised. Watching. Waiting.

"My body is a vessel. Use it."

Julian stepped forward

"There may be found upon us," Julian spoke, standing directly before April, outside of the triangle, facing her as her head bowed and her eyes closed. "Anyone that maketh his son or daughter pass through fire. An observer of times, an enchanter, a witch, a charmer, a consultant with familiar spirits, or a necromancer. These things are an abomination to the Lord, and Lord thy God will drive them out of here."

The whole room waited.

Waited.

And waited.

"I address you now, as the Spirit of the Lord is upon me, because he hath anointed me to heal the broken-hearted, to preach deliverance to the captives, and to preach the acceptable year of the Lord – so come forth. Use this vessel. Speak to us."

Julian looked back and forth. At the children leant up in the bed, peering at him. The doctors with clip boards held across their chest. The nurses, holding their crosses, tightly gripping pendants around their neck like their wellbeing was dependent upon it.

"Jesus came to free those under demon bondage, for whoever shall call upon the name of the Lord shall be saved – and I call upon the name of the Lord. And I shall be saved. And from the saved, I command you, use this vessel."

The candles flickered.

No one moved.

"I receive God's nature, and in his name, we command you, use this vessel. Tell us what your wish is."

April's eyes opened.

Everyone watched her.

Not just watched her – peered into her. Beheld her with such intensity that if eyes could pierce your flesh, she would be a bloody, skinless wreck.

Oscar sensed the danger.

He stood.

Julian held out his hand in a request that Oscar was to stay where he was.

Oscar halted. Watched. Waited.

April stood. Her eyes open, her pupils fully dilated, her

body hanging loose like a boneless animal. Like a ventriloquist's doll with only a loose guide propping her up.

"Demon," Julian continued. "You will remain within the triangle. In God's name, you will not leave it."

"Joanna," April mumbled.

"What?" Julian prompted. "Demon, repeat what you say."

April looked at a girl sitting up in bed behind Julian. The young girl's eyes were wide and alert, her body tensed, her young mind rendering her completely immobile.

"You will not leave that triangle, in God's name, you stand, and you tell us, who you—"

April stepped forward, out of the triangle made by the candles, and slowly stepped toward the young girl. Her bare feet made a gentle slap on the floor, the only sound that challenged the life machines – one of which was increasing in its frequency of beats. The one of the young girl April was stepping toward.

"Joanna…"

"You will stop! You will not move! You will—"

April sent her fist forward in a sudden, jolted movement. It settled into Julian's nose, which gave an audible crack as he fell back onto the floor.

Oscar was running immediately. Sprinting across the room, making his way toward her.

"Joanna…"

April approached the side of the girl. Barely older than seven. Her heart monitor was racing, her eyes ripped wide open, her body paralysed with illness and terror.

April reached her hand out toward the girl.

Oscar reached April's side and wrapped his arms around her chest.

"God, our Lord, King of ages," Oscar forced into her ear. "All-powerful and all-mighty, we beseech You to make powerless."

April's head rotated unnaturally, the only part of her body moving, twisting until it faced Oscar, inches from his desperate visage. In her eyes he saw nothing but black, nothing but terror.

This wasn't her.

This couldn't be her.

"You are powerless," its low, croaky voice whispered through April's mouth.

"Drive out every diabolic power, presence, and machination. Every evil influence, malefice, or evil eye and evil actions aimed against You."

"You think this will stop me?"

Oscar ignored it. He had to.

These things always said what they could to provoke.

He couldn't let it get to him.

He couldn't let it get April.

"Where there is envy and malice," he continued, "give us an abundance of goodness, endurance, and victory."

"I already have her."

"May You keep at bay and vanquish every evil power, every poison or malice invoked against us, by corrupt and envious demons."

"This has done nothing but bring forth the inevitable."

"Then, under the protection of Your authority, may we sing, in gratitude–"

"Your daughter is mine."

"–The Lord is my salvation!" Oscar screamed, his face scrunched up into a snarl, not letting it get to him, not letting its lies take him over. "Whom should I fear? I will not fear evil because You are with me!"

The demon's low chuckle forced her breath against him, stinking like rotting meat, and her body went limp. He caught her as she fell.

"My God, my strength," Oscar whispered as he took her to

the floor and waved a doctor over. "Lord of all peace. Father of all ages."

Julian began to sit up.

As the doctors descended on April, checking her pulse, checking her temperature, doing everything they needed to do to ensure her survival, Oscar turned to Julian, sat there nursing his wounded nose.

"Now," Oscar spat, "it is my turn to tell you how much of an idiot you are."

"Leave it out, Oscar. She's a big girl."

Oscar dove on top of Julian, grabbing his collar before he could stand.

"She does *not* belong to *you*! She is not your *pawn* you can use! She—"

"It's her," came a delicate voice.

Oscar stood and turned to the young girl. Startled, but speaking.

"I take it your name is Joanna," Oscar said. "Mine is Oscar."

"That was her. The thing that's been coming at night."

"Yes, I know. It was in her, now we've got rid of it, I promise—"

"No," the young girl insisted. "You don't understand. That is her face."

"What?"

Joanna dropped her head and refused to answer any more questions.

April had been lifted to a wheelchair and was being taken through the hospital. With a scowl at Julian, Oscar followed, taking her hand as he did.

THEN

27

IT WAS THE SAME ROUTINE. THE SAME CHAOS, THE SAME anarchy – but a new struggle.

As ever, Martin's exorcism consisted of flying furniture, shards of glass parading across the wind, lavish outbursts of elements that had no rational explanation.

And the girl, a young one, tied to a bed.

Only this time, Martin was on his own. When Derek had been there, they had worked together. They had battled the odds and made sure neither of them fell for the demon's taunts.

This time it wasn't so easy.

There was no respite. No point at which he could stand back and let someone else take over. No reassurance when he wondered if this would work.

"Soul of Christ, sanctify me!" Martin said, his voice trembling beneath his confidence. "Body of Christ, save me! Blood of Christ, inebriate me!"

He splashed holy water upon the writhing body beneath him, listening to the moans spew out of its wretched mouth with multiple pitches, each as unpleasant to the ear as the others.

The girl's face displayed numerous scabs. Cracked lips, bloodshot eyes, greasy hair – all of these were familiar sights to Martin. As was the blood around the crotch, the stains of urination over the bedsheets, and the wriggling of the body as its belly lifted into the air, rising upwards as it fought against is restraints.

But it was tougher. Those scabs were harder to look at, the blood harder to clean off, and the dried urine a smell impossible to escape.

He refused to think it. He wasn't going to wish Derek was there. He wasn't going to waste another thought on him. He would not.

Though he knew he could not do this alone.

"Water for the side of Christ, wash me!" he persevered. "Passion of Christ, strengthen me! Banish all of the forces of evil from me, destroy them, vanish them, so this house can be healthy and full of good deeds!"

A booming, croaky laughter sprang from the depths of the poor girl's throat and pushed itself to the surface of her lips. It filled the room, floating along the chaos, the bed quivering along the floor.

"You fool…" the demon's voice spoke, in at least five pitches and five distinct accents.

Martin would not listen. He knew better than that.

He had been taught not to listen.

"Burn all these evils in hell, that they may never again touch me, touch this house, or touch this girl, or any creature in the world!"

The demon's laughter announced itself once more.

"You never should have done this…" it claimed.

"I command and bid all the power who molest me!"

"Molest you?" The demon choked on its laughter. "The devil molests your mother in hell…"

It shook him for a second. The words, they made him pause. But he continued.

"By the power of God all powerful, in the name of our Saviour, leave this girl forever and be consigned to everlasting hell."

A sadistic grin spread wider than a grin could naturally spread.

"You never should have done this…"

"Lord, you said you give us peace, and peace you give us. Give us that peace now."

"You never should have done this… without *him*."

Martin faltered.

She was right.

She's right? Get a grip.

A demon was never right. That's what Derek always reminded him – it was never right about what it said, only right in its choice of insecurities it senses.

"We may be liberated from every evil–"

"He's going to *die*, you know."

"We may be liberated from every–"

"You should have used him, but he's going to *die*."

"We may be liberated–"

"And you aren't going to be there because you're a selfish little boy."

"*Shut up!*"

Martin regretted his outburst as soon as the scream had scorched his throat, and the demon's cocky laughter only made it worse.

"The devil has decided on its vengeance."

"Shut up," Martin repeated – this time as more of a beg than a command.

"Lamia will return."

"Please, just shut up."

Martin's head dropped. He covered his face.

What am I doing?

"You know it wasn't his fault; now look what's happened to you."

Martin shook his head profusely. Why was he listening to this? He knew better.

But this had been inside of him for a while. This wasn't just a taunt.

It was the truth.

"We are going to implant spawn," the demon continued with a singsong voice. "We are going to implant a demon child, and Lamia is going to infect it, and Derek is going to suffer to the last."

Martin fled the room. He pounded down the stairs and out of the house.

He ignored the family of the girl behind him, waiting to see if he'd had success.

He hadn't had success.

He wasn't going to have success.

Not without Derek.

Derek, of whom the demon had just revealed its intentions.

Martin would try to let Derek know. He'd try to contact him. He'd ring him, even show up at his old apartment.

But, just as Derek had promised in their last phone call, Martin would struggle to find him.

He vowed he'd persist. That he'd find him.

Somehow.

NOW

28

FOLDED ARMS, DEADLY FROWN, AND FURIOUS EYES. OSCAR DID not disguise his anger from Julian one bit. If anything, he was ready to stand up to him, once and for all.

It had been too far.

"Honestly," Julian insisted. "She agreed to it. She insisted she could do it."

"Then you should have said no."

"In hindsight, yes, but–"

"To hell with hindsight!" Oscar said, standing up and throwing his arms into the air.

He'd had a few days to calm down, but he was still livid. April was fast asleep in their bedroom, and Oscar had reluctantly agreed to let Julian round to say his piece.

He wasn't at all interested in Julian's piece.

There were far heavier thoughts weighing down Oscar's mind.

"Look, children are dying, it was a tough call to make. And I gave her the decision entirely. I'm surprised she didn't talk it through with you."

"I'm not," Oscar blankly stated.

"What do you mean?"

Oscar went to speak, then found himself lost for words. He sat down on the edge of a seat, ran his hands through his hair, focussing on the corner of the room and staring at it.

"Oscar, what's troubling you?" Julian asked.

"Like you care."

"I do care."

Oscar grimaced at Julian. "You've been a dick to me since the moment you met me. I thought that would change after the prison, but ever since we've announced the pregnancy, you've come back more dickish than normal."

"I suppose I was just thinking about the strain it could put on the business."

"No, Julian, you were thinking about *yourself*. As always."

Julian pulled out a chair and sat beside Oscar. He allowed a few moments of reflective quiet to pass, allowing himself to mull over the words that had been said. Oscar kept his gaze fixed on the corner of the room.

"Maybe you're right," Julian admitted. "Maybe."

Oscar scoffed.

"What do you want from me?" Julian joked. "It's what I do. But honestly, I can see there's something troubling you. Something *else* troubling you. And I'm here to help. Really."

Oscar wiped his hands over his face, wondering if he should really confide in Julian. But who else was there? Derek was ill. His parents didn't particularly understand these things. It felt like his only option.

Fine.

If only for Julian's expertise.

"It's April," Oscar said. "She's been acting strange all the way through this pregnancy. Like, really strange."

"It's hormones, surely? I mean, pregnant women sometimes do crazy stuff."

"No, it's… other stuff."

"Have you been to the doctor's?"

"Yes."

"What did they say?"

"That these things were normal."

"Well there you go!"

Oscar stood, paced a few steps, then stopped and turned to Julian.

"But it all seems too strange."

"You think there's something paranormal at work?"

"Yes!"

"That's fair. You've seen too much; that's always going to be in your mind. But when there's a rational explanation, you still go with that one. And if the doctors are saying it's fine, then you've got a rational explanation."

"But what about... Anna?"

Even after everything that happened, Oscar still struggled to approach the subject, knowing how difficult it was for Julian. But Julian gulped, took a mature stance, and continued.

"Yes, I know. But that was an anomaly. You know how many of these possible hauntings we've been to actually turn out to be hauntings?"

"Jeeze. Less than five percent?"

"Far less. Are you sure it's not just you being paranoid?"

Oscar sighed. Folded his arms.

Julian had a point.

But it couldn't be so simple. It just couldn't.

"Right, let me tell you what's happened, and we'll see if you think it sounds like something," Oscar decided.

"Okay, go for it."

Oscar drew a breath, preparing himself.

"When she met my parents, and we were eating – I mean, April has a go at me if I so much as open my mouth slightly for a second with it full. She devoured a chicken with her mouth without even thinking."

"Okay," Julian acknowledged.

"She bleeds. So much she has to wear sanitary towels every day. She bled in Mothercare, after staring out a kid, then passed out."

"And the doctors said?"

"That it's rare, but happens. But, still. She's nasty toward kids. And, what the demon said to me the other day."

"You know they'll say anything to taunt you."

"Yes, but she said – the demon said it already has her. That my daughter is hers."

"Because it was a demon, Oscar; that's what they do. Demons are dickheads. They try to say nasty stuff."

"But – she whispered Latin in her sleep. And I translated it, and it–"

"April has used Latin a lot in her work. If she spoke it in her sleep then, honestly, it wouldn't surprise me."

Oscar bowed his head, collected himself, and sat down.

"So you really think it's nothing?" he asked.

"Oh, I don't think it's nothing," Julian responded. "I think it's a pregnant woman, who's perhaps an extreme example. I don't think there's a single thing demonic or paranormal about it."

"Really?"

"Really. And I think you need to relax."

Oscar nodded.

"Thanks. You're right, I guess."

"I'm glad I could help."

After a few moments, Julian reassured him once more, and said his goodbyes. Oscar walked through to the bedroom and watched April, watching as her chest slowly rose in her sleep, as her belly remained still, as she stayed at peace.

Maybe Julian was right.

The guy was a knob, but he did have an irritating habit of accuracy.

Maybe Oscar was being paranoid.

He lay beside her. Stroked her hair off her face. Placed his arm around her chest.

He slowly drifted off to sleep. All the time, ignoring those words coming out of April's mouth in a subdued whisper.

"Filea mea. Filea mea. Filea mea."

Eventually, they turned to dead, distant noise, and he dreamt of nothing but his happy family and his healthy, wonderful daughter.

(1 MONTH)

29

APRIL WAS HUNGRY. RAVENOUS. FAMISHED.

She could quite easily eat two dinners; that was how hungry she was.

She was fully aware that she was eating for two, and that the bump, growing ever bigger, needed more and more energy.

Not that it felt bereft of energy; it wriggled and bashed like it was having a rave in a cage! She had seen possessed victims having seizures that would likely cause less of a raucous in her belly.

But, such was the cost of pregnancy. In a month, she would arrive.

In a month, *it* would arrive.

She wiped a backhand of sweat from her forehead, then irritably dabbed it against her coat. She was sweltering. What's more, she knew that her humungous belly was creeping out from below her top – something she had always found quite gross in pregnant women. But, in that moment, she truly, unequivocally, unobtrusively, did not care. It needed to be released from the sweaty restraints of her top that was becoming more and more fitted by the day.

She huffed.

God, I'm ages away.

It was going to take her at least fifteen minutes to walk home, and that would have been without the extra load. She regretted telling Oscar she'd be fine, that she just wanted a walk, just to expend some energy. She wanted that boy there to carry her home. Or, at the minimum, drive her.

Glancing at a newsagent as she hobbled past, she felt her pockets for change.

Nothing. Nada. Zilch.

Not even anything for a packet of Freddos.

But, surely, they would not deny a pregnant woman a packet of Freddos?

I mean, what kind of psychopath are they?

She paused by a lamp post, reaching her arm out to support herself as she leant against it. Spotting a nearby park bench she wobbled from side to side, meandering her way over and plodding her expanded arse cheeks against the rusty seat.

A huge huff pushed out of her mouth.

I would murder for food.

A fluffy sensation brushed against her bare shin – a shin that hadn't been so bare a few weeks ago. How was it that even her shins were getting bigger? She had always been petite, and she knew she still was deep down, but as she gazed upon her body she saw nothing but excess skin pushed to its limits.

Her eyes wandered downwards, and the fluffy sensation appeared in the form of a cat. Its eyes peered upwards, somberly reaching out to her with innocent, wide eyes.

She reached a hand down and brushed it across the cat's soft yet bristly fur. The feline closed its eyes as if to hint at its enjoyment in response to the attention it was receiving.

April was sure that, if the cat had the ability, it would be smiling.

There's always something a little magically triumphant in

the ability to win the affection of a stranger's cat. Like, because that cat likes you, it means the whole world should deem you superior.

She pressed down more with her strokes, feeling its body press under the pressure, knowing that the cat would appreciate a rougher approach. Which it did. It lay down, flopped on its side, and rolled onto its back in order to expose its belly.

April tickled the cat's belly, watching as she or he closed its eyes once more and let its paws flop to the side in appreciation. It was lapping up the attention, and April was loving it.

She sniggered to herself. If only taking care of a newborn child was going to be this simple. She'd had enough unwarranted stories from anyone she knew with a child about what hell the first few months are. So much so, she was starting to wonder why any of them bothered in the first place, if it was such a treacherous time.

The hunger pain returned with a vengeance. A sharp pang in her empty stomach, sticking against her skin with a sharpened edge.

She looked down at the cat as it rubbed its head against her hands, fussing her with further unprecedented enthusiasm.

She placed a hand around its neck.

She placed her other hand around its legs.

She lifted the kitten up to her mouth.

Its confused eyes turned sombrely toward her, as if awaiting some kind of explanation. It anticipated the next round of fussing, the next tickle on the neck, the next rub on the belly.

That affection, however, was not forthcoming.

April gripped her hands tightly, so tight there was no way the cat could escape. It wriggled against the pressure of its neck, but such was her strength it found itself almost immovable.

April opened her jaw, prepared her teeth, and exposed the cat's belly toward her. With mouthful of anticipatory saliva, she sunk her teeth into the belly of the kitten, clamping down with all her might.

The cat moaned a long, unpleasant, high-pitched meow that only seemed to pick up aggression the more she bit.

But the cat couldn't move. April had clamped her hands too tightly.

She took her face away, chewed the first few mouthfuls until they were ready to swallow, then sunk them down her throat and into her belly.

Wiping some blood off her lips and onto her sleeve, she dug her teeth in once more.

The fur was annoying. It was a bit prickly against the top of her mouth, and it made her quite irritable for a moment. Then she allowed the flesh underneath to batter back and forth across her tongue, allowing it to shrink under the chewing of her jaw, and relished the flavour.

She lifted her head back.

Licked her lips, ensuring that she got every droplet before it fell down her chin.

She couldn't waste a bite.

She closed her eyes, feeling the pieces slip down her chest, feeling them feed her, give her energy, give her spawn energy.

When she next turned to the cat, its body had fallen limp.

How disgusting.

There was no way she was going to eat a limp cat.

She dumped it on the ground, discarded it, and made the jaunty walk home, feeling far better fed.

30

DEREK'S INCESSANT INSISTENCE THAT GOOD WOULD PREVAIL HAD been a major source of irritation to Julian, yes – but what he'd give to have him back at his full ability at that very moment.

He'd been at this case of the children's ward too long, and he was running out of ideas.

It was rare that one gets to a point in their life where they must decisively conclude – *I am completely and utterly stuck.*

It is typical that one should use a cliché to sum up such a feeling, so you'd have to forgive Julian's mind for forging a number of them together – but he knew that everyone, in their lives, comes to a crossroad. Everyone rolls the dice, and everyone sees a number come up that they do not wish to see.

Some people may even think they are stuck, but they aren't – they just aren't aware that either there is a solution upon their next stumble, or that there isn't a solution to present itself at all. Once they decide there will be no way going forward, they move on. They come to terms with it, and they readjust.

Julian could do no such thing.

Children were dying, and more children were at risk of death.

This wasn't a situation where Julian could throw in the figurative towel. This was a solution where he had to pick up that towel, look at it from all angles, examine it, and continue to hypothesise and test until he was blue in the face.

But what else could he suggest? Where else could he turn?

He had given Jason all of his 'I supposes and all of his 'I reckons – and he was out.

As he twisted in the chair in Derek's study, mindlessly rotating, spinning until his mind turned to a static race, he wished an answer would present itself to him. That an answer would throw itself into his lap. That it would give him something that would at least allow him to go to sleep. His mind needed rest, but until it reached a conclusion, it would not stop.

It was too dangerous to put April back in that position. She almost lost it before – and, what's more, that reluctant decision to encourage her to act as a conduit had not paid off.

He slowed down the spinning of the chair.

Or had it?

She had taunted Oscar. She had said, "I already have her." Followed by, "Your daughter is mine."

Logically, the demon would know it had a daughter…

He'd told Oscar never to listen to a demon's taunts. It was one of the greatest lessons Derek had ever taught him.

But the more he thought about it, the more something didn't feel right.

Or was he just trying to use the demon's words to provide a solution? Was he so lost that he was making them out of nothing? Was he so lost that–

He saw something.

Whilst mindlessly spinning himself around on the chair, his eyes passed a vague blur in the bookshelf. Something small, a glimmer, something that didn't fit.

Behind the first layer of books on the bookcase that took up the vast amount of the wall, the dark-brown tint of the shelves mixed with the shadows of the second and third layer of books. But, in a flicker of light that caught a narrow gap as he spun, there was something discoloured. Something light brown. Something...

He leapt from his chair, grabbing books and throwing them out of the way. Derek would be fuming if he saw Julian treating his books this way, but if there was something in this bookshelf he had yet seen, something...

A brown piece of parchment, folded up more times than would be natural, was wedged behind a set of books. Behind the third layer, hidden away where someone did not intend it to be found.

Julian pulled the parchment out. He held it before him and read the message scrawled barely legibly on the front.

EXCERPT REMOVED *from Derek Lansdale's journal.*

JULIAN HAD READ Derek's journals – he'd studied them front to back, especially when learning about The Edward King War. Those were things he needed to know.

But he'd never realised that there were missing pages.

He unravelled the piece of parchment, and read each word quickly yet carefully.

27TH DECEMBER 2008

I WRITE this journal entry with a heavy heart, and thoughts full of regret. I feared writing this entry, unable to decide whether it was necessary. But I swore these records would be kept. I swore I would make note of what I know so that the world could be burdened with the knowledge when it was ready, or when it was needed.

BUT IT IS with great solace, and a troublesome mind, that my pen makes these scribbles upon the page.

I'M NOT EVEN ENTIRELY sure where to start. Outside my window, people are taking down wreaths. Packing away Christmas lights. Boxing their presents and taking them to their storage.

I AM NOT TAKING down any wreaths, lights, or boxing any presents. Because I never put any up. Nor did I receive any in the first place. Because I was busy. Working a case.

THE CASE in question is that of Madelina Esteves. A Portuguese woman in her early twenties, working in the United Kingdom as a nurse. She changed her location to Edinburgh, Scotland, as she was seeking me out. Seeking me to help her.

MADELINA WAS PREGNANT. But with what?

NO MEDICAL REASON existed for her frequent troubles.

SHE SAID it started with a need for meat. She would find a piece of chicken, or a raw steak, and she would devour it. Rip it off the bone with her teeth. Tear it to shreds until its contents were smeared over her cheeks.

. . .

THEN CAME *the aggressive sexual urges. She would regularly have sexual encounters, then wake up the next morning with no recollection, with the only knowledge of what she had done being the marks on her lover's neck.*

HER MORNING SICKNESS *continued as per any normal pregnancy. But she found that she was passing objects she did not remember swallowing. Most notable were a set of rosary beads, and a crucifix.*

SHE WOULD BE *aggressive toward children, taunting them, even threatening them.*

SHE WOULD BLEED *from the vagina at regular intervals. The doctors told her this happened sometimes, but the baby was healthy and fine. But it kept happening. She said it got to the point that she wore a sanitary towel each day, and would have to replace it every hour, such was the frequency of the blood.*

AND THERE WAS *a constant murmur of Latin whilst she was unconscious, one that would chill anyone who was in the presence of her weary, sleeping body.*

THESE SYMPTOMS *all may sound like extreme hormones, or delusions. This is what she was diagnosed with.*

. . .

I wasn't sure. I just wasn't sure. All of these things were, without a doubt, extreme – but could there be a rational explanation?

I wasn't sure. Until two weeks ago.

When she killed a child.

I knew then that there was something at work. My research led me to Lamia – a child-eating demon of Greek mythology.

But by the time I got to her it was too late.

She had descended on an orphanage. The sight that my eyes bestowed themselves upon will never leave me. Never. It was carnage. Reckless, unequivocal carnage.

Pieces of children lay about the house. Some of the bodies were unrecognisable. At times, you weren't even sure what you were looking at – whether it was intestines, muscles, or whatever else. It was sick. There is no other way to describe the mental image permanently tattooed onto the forefront of my mind. Sick. It was completely sick.

I found Madelina standing on the edge of a hill, facing a steep drop to her death.

. . .

I KNEW this baby could be saved. I knew that there was a way. She was days away from giving birth.

BUT SHE WAS ADAMANT.

YES, I have saved a great many people, but this is the case that will stay in my mind.

I HAD to believe good would win. Because it normally does. It always does. I know it.

BUT THIS TIME...

THIS ENTRY WILL NOT RESIDE in my normal journal. It can't.

IT IS with great regret that I can't allow this to be common knowledge, and that I will be removing this page. If this is you, Martin, reading this, then I sincerely apologise for my cowardly actions.

IF THIS IS NOT Martin reading this, then I am still sorry to place the curse of knowledge upon you. Especially as the reason you've found this is because I have no ability to stop you – meaning that I am likely to be in a position that I can not respond to your questions or disappointment.

. . .

THIS IS a demon we can't defeat the normal way. This is a demon that can't be exorcised – it is not taking over a body, it is living within it. It is a child waiting to be born. But that child can still be good.

WE HAVE TO BELIEVE THAT.

THERE IS ALWAYS A SOLUTION. Always a way. Always something we can do.

THAT CHILD COULD HAVE BEEN BORN good. If only we'd have believed it.

I SIGN off from this note with great regret for my failures, in hope that you will not make the same.

YOURS IN SPIRIT,

DEREK LANSDALE

THE HANDS that held the parchment shook.

Julian's arms trembled. His thoughts distorted. His eyes not knowing where to look.

Who was Martin?

Julian buried such a question to the back of his mind and recalled a recent interaction he'd had with Oscar. A conversation where he'd reassured Oscar of all the things that he'd seen – where he'd reassured Oscar they were nothing.

Pregnant. Like Madelina.

The bleeds, just like Madelina.

The obsession with children, just like Madelina.

The whispering Latin in her sleep, just like…

Oh, God.

April.

31

HAVING SPENT HIS ENTIRE DRIVING LIFE OBEYING EVERY SPEED limit and braking for every turn – something that Julian was fully aware incensed the driver's stuck behind him, but insisted was the right choice, as it was safe – meant that his conscience was rejecting every action of his speedy, erratic driving. His breathing became so heavy he verged on hyperventilating, his arms shook like he was being charged with an electric volt, and his heart pounded like it was going to burst out of his chest.

He didn't care.

He had taken April off the streets. He'd found her. Shown her what it was to be a Sensitive. He had cared for her, been the big brother she needed, and had produced a damn fine, head-strong woman out of it.

He couldn't let whatever that thing inside of her was take control of her.

The thought was one he couldn't even bear. It brought tears to his eyes to even contemplate her demise, or even that she would be caused any pain.

After a half-hour drive spent clutching the steering wheel

and hoping for the best, he brought the car to a rough halt and leapt out of the door. Not caring whether it was locked or not, he made his way up the path to April and Oscar's flat, peering through the windows as he did.

All the curtains appeared to be drawn.

He pounded his fist against the door, feeling it battle against its hinges, and waited.

Nothing.

He pounded his fist against it once more, shouting her name.

"April! April!"

Nothing.

He placed his hand on the door handle, ready to barge the door down, only to find the door surprisingly unlocked. A gentle push sent it creaking open into a dark, lifeless corridor.

He stepped inside. Closed the door behind him. Edged his way forward.

"April?" he shouted, hoping she would respond.

Hoping *April* would respond.

Not something ungodly stuck inside of her.

"April, are you there?"

He used the walls for a guide, his legs inching across the carpet, until he came to the opening of the living room.

"April?"

A sudden jump impacted his body as he saw her. He poised in the doorway, taken aback by the calmness of the room.

She sat in a chair. Not a rocking chair so much, but a smaller chair that allowed her to sink deeply into it, and allowed her to rock slowly forward, then back, with such a slight movement that if it weren't accompanied by a sinister creak, Julian wouldn't even be sure he saw it.

"April?" he asked, quietly, almost worried he was going to wake some kind of beast, or already be engaging with it.

April did not look demonic. She did not look possessed, wretched, or any kind of destitute. But there was something worrying, an undertone of disconcerting eeriness, in the way that she stroked her belly. She allowed her large, pregnant bump to proudly pronounce itself in all its nudity from beneath her top. Her hands brushed up and down, up and down, up and down, with such a gentle nurture that it was like she was protecting a precious item she had stolen and did not want to be disturbed.

"April," Julian spoke, "I just wanted to check on you. See if you are okay."

"I'm fine, Julian," she answered nonchalantly. "How are you?"

"Yeah, I'm good. I'm good."

"How's the case on the children's ward coming along?"

The first true pang of fear sent a shiver sprinkling up his spine.

If she was the one who had done it, then God knows how he was supposed to answer.

He edged slowly forward. Trying to get closer. He knew his crucifix was in his back pocket. He kept one hand behind his back so he was able to withdraw it at any time.

"I don't know, April," Julian replied. "Really struggling, I guess."

"Oh, I don't believe that."

He edged forward.

"Why not?"

"Wouldn't be the first time you lied to me."

"When have I ever lied to you, April?"

"I don't know. Right now?"

"How am I lying to you now?"

"Because you seem to be hiding a cross behind your back."

He stopped edging. His feet stuck to the floor like his trainers were part of the carpet. He was poised between attack and defence. Between getting the cross and going full pelt, or being cautious, as he did not know how much she knew.

"So, where's Oscar?"

"Oscar? Oh, he's out. Gone to get me some food."

"Oh yeah, what you eating nowadays?"

The side of her mouth lifted into a grin.

"What you are getting at, Julian?"

She continued to rock. Continued to stroke her belly. Continued to act so, so strangely.

There was only one thing Julian knew.

If this was April's ship, she wasn't the one steering it.

"I'm not getting at anything."

"Then get rid of the cross. You're freaking me out."

That was it.

He had to move.

He had to do something.

He flung the cross out from behind him – but, before he could present it or begin any kind of incantation, he found himself lifted into the air. His throat tightened, his chest rose, and his fingers shook until the cross fell to the floor.

April didn't falter. Didn't so much as blink. She simply remained, gently rocking, stroking her belly.

"April…" Julian whimpered between chokes. "Please…"

Like a bolt of wind punching him in his chest, he was taken off his feet, sent soaring out of the room until he reached the back wall of the cupboard.

He sat, slumped beneath a mop, his head spinning.

He couldn't make sense of it.

His head was groggy. His vision a blur.

His head smacked once more against the wall behind him. Then again. Then again. He tried to resist it, but he couldn't; something he couldn't see was pushing against his head too hard. Eventually, his awareness depleted to the point that he wasn't even able to acknowledge his head slamming against the back wall any longer.

The last thing he saw before he passed out was the closet door slamming shut, and April still sitting in her chair.

Rocking.

Stroking.

32

Oscar greeted the strange silence of his house as an infrequent occurrence. Normally, the moans and bustles of a pregnant woman would occupy the small rooms of their cohabited flat, but as he returned home in the darkness of late evening, it felt unusual to return to the quiet nights he and April used to have.

I suppose that will all change now.

In weeks, maybe even days to come, a new member of their family would greet them.

Family.

It felt strange to think it.

He wasn't just with a girlfriend anymore. He was with his family. His perfect life he could never have envisaged. He was the man of the house – the protector.

Although he knew April was far tougher than he, he still allowed himself a small smile at the thought.

He turned the key and stepped on that day's mail. He picked it up and sifted through the envelopes. Once he'd noticed they were all bills, he placed them beside the shoe rack and made his way through the hall to the only place that was lit.

The kitchen.

As soon as he entered, a wonderful aroma of perfectly cooked food took him aback. Just the right meld of bread and meat, combining into a perfect harmony of smells that made his mouth salivate in anticipation.

April sat at the table, smiling warmly toward him. Her hands caressed her exposed belly with small strokes, and a dish was placed in front of the empty seat beside her.

"Wow," Oscar said. "Is this for me?"

"Of course."

"But – you haven't got anything?"

"I've had mine. I just wanted to treat you."

Oscar looked playfully back at her.

It was lovely, but… odd.

It wasn't that April wasn't generous; in fact, quite the opposite. And it wasn't that the look on her face pierced through his eyes with an unsettling quality. Nor was it that there was no food in front of her. It was just…

She never willingly cooked. She had barely spoken to him over the difficulties of her pregnancy. He had felt isolated and alone, and this was a huge surprise.

"I – I don't know what to say," Oscar honestly admitted.

"I just wanted to do something," April told him with a calm, soothing texture that he wasn't used to in her voice. "Something to say thank you, to say I know how hard these nine months have been."

"Well, I… I'm speechless."

He hastily removed his jacket and sat at his place at the table. The dish below him, accompanied by a side plate adorning fresh, warmed bread, held a meat soup of the perfect colour, the perfect steamy temperature, and the perfect presentation.

He dipped his spoon, letting it sink, then bringing out a spoonful of liquid with a slice of meat, which he placed in his mouth and chewed. It was so fine. A delicacy one could only achieve with expertise in cooking. It was even still warm, but not so much that it would burn your mouth.

"Oh, wow," Oscar said. "This is amazing."

April said nothing.

She just watched him.

Watched as he took another spoonful and enjoyed the delightful taste of this home-prepared food.

Then he stopped.

Paused.

Wait.

This wasn't right. This whole situation, this whole scenario – it wasn't right. April barely liked putting pre-made pie and chips into the oven. She had never made something from scratch. How was it she had made something that tasted so perfect?

And how was it the right temperature just as he happened to enter the room?

"What's going on, April?" he asked. "You hate cooking. You can barely do anything with a saucepan. How did you make this?"

She shrugged her shoulders like it was nothing, not taking her eyes away from her precious belly.

"I'm going to be a mother. Time to learn to be a bit more motherly."

"I don't get it, this, just – it's delightful, don't get me wrong. I..."

He struggled for the words. Tried to snatch them as they floated around his head. But they were not forthcoming.

He couldn't articulate what was wrong, it was just...

Something.

"Please, have the rest," she insisted.

Reluctantly, he dipped his spoon once more, and continued

to eat the rest. She didn't take her eyes from him, watching him with a sly smile the whole time.

"No," April grunted.

Oscar's head abruptly lifted.

April's face had changed. The smile was gone. She looked distressed.

"I said no."

"April?"

She turned around, placing her back toward him.

What was she on about?

"Said no to what?"

"I know you said it wouldn't kill him, I know you said it, but I can't, I can't…"

"April?"

Oscar stood, cautiously stepping toward her, his hand reaching out.

"Just let him live… Let him live and I'll do what you want…"

"April, what's going on?"

"Please, just leave him… I love him…"

"April?"

"I'll give birth to it now, if you just leave him…"

"April?"

April's face turned toward him. For the first time in months, he saw her eyes, her lost expression. Tears cascaded down her cheeks.

Her belly had gone completely red. It was kicking.

More than kicking.

It was throbbing. In multiple places, lumps came and went, quickening in pace.

"April, what's–"

His words got lost.

His vision unfocussed.

"I'm sorry, Oscar."

He fell to his knees.

"I'm so, so sorry."

He collapsed to the floor.

For a few seconds, he stared at her feet.

The throbbing lumps concentrated their attention on the lower part of her belly, reaching for him, as if trying to get at him.

He tried to say her name.

He tried. Even tried reaching out for her.

But he didn't manage to utter a syllable before his mind relinquished his consciousness to the depths of a blackout.

His hand stretched out, then flopped.

April was ready to give birth.

33

Luxuries.

They are things that we take for granted.

The luxury of food. Home. Family. Our working limbs. Our functional brains.

Then we have luxuries we afford ourselves. A fancy dinner out, a trip to the cinema with snacks, or buying that book you've been wanting for ages.

To Derek, life was the luxury he could feel slipping away.

Each breath seemed to take effort. Each move increased his struggling heartbeat. Each thought was thinking that it may be his last.

And as he lay there, attached to machines, staring groggily at the ceiling above, he could feel what the children were talking about.

They felt it because they were close to death. They saw it because they were close. For when we walk the tightrope between life and death, we can see both sides spinning beneath us. He'd been to hell. It was many, many years ago, but he had. Twice. He'd seen what it had to offer. And that feeling, that flickering flame lashing at his skin, that sense of dread that every step took, even the distant screams vibrating his prickly skin – he could feel it once more. Coming closer.

The entity in the children's ward had spread to the corridor, spread to his room. Its presence lingered there, but its body did not.

He'd witnessed Lamia before. He knew what it was after. And the children's ward was the perfect place. Souls that can't fight. Faces that would see Lamia in its true form – not the face of the host Lamia chose, but its true from. It relished the sight of vulnerable targets as their face melded into horror at the true form of the beast relinquishing that child from life.

That demon had chosen an orphanage before.

Now its next target was the children's ward.

He wanted to jump up and warn them. To rush into the other room, scream that they should arm themselves, begin the rites of exorcism. But his thoughts put so much of a strain on his weary head that the actual actions themselves may just be the very actions that removed the final breath from his body.

His head dropped to its side. The muscle in his neck strained.

Where was Julian?

Death was waiting around the corner. He had so much unfinished. So many thoughts, words, and lessons.

If he died doing it, he would insist to Julian his final lesson. Would batter this lesson into Julian's head until he could do nothing but agree. Would force him to hear it.

Good will always prevail.

He drifted out of consciousness, barely able to notice the nurse as she came in to check on him. He was awoken to the news that he needed to eat. She gave him morphine and adrenaline to help him sit up.

He barely touched the cheap, cold pie the hospital had brought to him.

"We have a visitor for you," the nurse told him. "A friend."

Good.

Julian.

He needed to know that Julian would not remain the cynic he was. He needed to know–

It was not Julian.

It was not human.

Lamia's true form unveiled itself. Long hair above elf ears, a naked torso trickling lines of blood down its naked breasts and to its waist, where a long, slithering snake tail took the place of its legs.

But this demon was not the size of a person, nor was it standing before him. It was far smaller than that. It hovered off the ground. Asleep. Its limbs entwined into a circle.

The size of a new born baby. The height of a woman's womb. Curled into a foetal position.

This demon was not hovering in the air.

There was something around it.

A body.

Walking into the room.

The nurse smiled at the body. Where the head would be. Welcomed it into his room.

"Hello, Derek," came a soothing voice. "Don't worry, I'm not interested in you."

What?

Its legs came out of the shadow.

Its belly.

Its face.

April.

Its face was April.

He finally saw what had been in Madelina. What had forced her to eat those children. What had killed those children. And was now within April.

Hidden in the unborn baby of a pregnant woman's womb.

But that child could be saved. He was sure of it.

194

That child yet to be born was home to the demon. It could be exorcized. Surely.

The nurse insisted it was time for rest and Derek reluctantly obliged, falling asleep in the midst of his objections.

He woke later to the terrible shrieks and mass hysterics that indicated a young girl called Joanna had been killed.

34

A STREAM OF PROJECTILE VOMITING AWOKE OSCAR FROM HIS daze. Once the shock of his rude awakening had diminished, he wiped perspiration from his brow and attempted to adjust his mind to his surroundings.

He sat up in the darkness of a small, cramped space. Faint light seeped through the outline of a door.

He was in a cupboard.

He stood, turned on the light.

A sudden lurch from his body brought up another mouthful of the soup April had made for him, forcing him to spew poison over a pair of stray shoes he hadn't worn in a while.

"Oscar?" came a faint voice.

He spun around.

Julian lay on the ground, rubbing his head

"Julian?"

"Oscar…" Julian's distant eyes became abruptly alert as the dawn of realisation announced itself on his face. "Oh my God, April! April! Oscar, April, she–"

"I know."

Oscar could see Julian's eyes flicker as his thoughts raced.

"Oscar…" Julian's weary face mulled over a set of difficult words. "I don't know if we can save her."

"We can."

"We don't know–"

"We're both still alive, aren't we?"

Julian nodded.

"She spoke to it, I heard her," Oscar continued. "She argued with it."

"But she–"

"Julian – we are both *alive*. If she didn't want us alive, then that poison would have killed me, not just knocked me out. She's still in there."

Julian's phone beeped.

He snatched it from his pocket and brought it to his eyes, recoiling in despair as he read a text message.

"What is it?" Oscar asked.

"Another child has died at the hospital," Julian answered.

They shared a look of understanding. They knew who the murderer was.

"Help me get this door open," Oscar demanded.

Julian used the wall to steady himself to his feet. They stood back and barged the door together, managing to burst it open on the fourth attempt.

They both fell to the floor, still dizzy from their unconscious states.

"We need to get to the hospital," Julian stated. "Derek's fought this thing before. We need to talk to him and go from there."

Julian turned to Oscar. Saw the look on his face. A lost boy, scared, and worried.

"Julian…" Oscar whispered.

A tear edged out the corner of his eyes and announced itself on his cheek, glistening in the moonlight.

"I know," Julian said. "I know. But we are going to find her."

"But, my daughter…"

"We'll find her too. I promise."

Dragging Oscar by the arm, Julian took him out of the house and to his car. They sped to the hospital in silence, both of them too tense to talk.

By the time they pulled up, Oscar had managed to achieve a feigned sense of composure. Enough to be able to run the whole way to the children's ward.

35

DEREK HAD RECOILED AT THE MEMORY OF THE BLOODY STATE OF the children's ward.

The sight of April in his room. The appearance of the evil hidden within her. The screams that followed minutes after.

He hadn't wanted to see what April had done.

No – he hadn't wanted to see what *Lamia* had done.

But he'd had to.

The walls of the children's ward had been decorated in blood like never before. A mutilated body ripped to pieces of unidentifiable meat, spread over the bed and floor. But it didn't stop there; the spectacle had found itself onto every wall. Splashes of red stuck to the laughing faces of clowns and happy childish images. The floor was wet with red, and doctors were seeing to nurses who had been injured in the crossfire.

This felt bigger.

Like it was building up to something.

Like this was nearly the end.

Derek was sat up when Oscar and Julian ran into his room, eating a disgusting cream-coloured dish of hospital food.

"Derek, have you seen April?" Julian asked.

"I have not."

"Derek, I know. I know who Lamia is. I know what it did to the pregnant woman before."

"What?" exclaimed Oscar. "What happened?"

"It's got April, hasn't it?"

"What's got April?" Oscar persisted. "Who is it?"

Julian hesitantly turned to Oscar and told him who Lamia was. What the demon had done to Madelina. What Madelina had done to the orphanage.

As the initial shock subsided, Oscar's mind bombarded him with numerous unhelpful thoughts. As Derek watched Oscar, he could almost see the image of April clear in his thoughts, tearing children's skin from their bones with her teeth, much like she had the chicken. Watching her as she tore the children's ward apart.

"Where can we find her?" Oscar shot at Derek.

Derek shrugged his shoulders.

"Bloody hell, Derek, this is April!" Oscar rushed to his side. "Where woud she go? *Where?*"

"Oscar–" Julian tried to interject.

"Where would she go? Tell me, Derek, bloody tell me!"

Julian put his arms across Oscar and coerced him away from Derek.

"He is really sick, Oscar," Julian spoke in a low voice. "You're not going to get anywhere like this."

"Fine!" Oscar barked, throwing Julian's hands off him. He took to Derek's bedside as slow as his shaking, speeding body would allow him. "Help us What do you know?"

Derek's mouth opened slowly and his words came out with difficulty.

"The child… can be saved."

"What?"

"The child is possessed, not her. But it still can be saved." Derek looked to Julian. "Good can win against it. It can."

"How do we find her?" Julian asked.

"I… don't know."

Oscar's hands ran through his hair.

"Where should we start looking?" Julian demanded, insisting that Derek should have something to help.

"Look… for places that mean something to you…"

Oscar nodded, thought, his mind jumping through all the locations he had ever been to.

"The pharmacy!" he decided. "That's where we first met."

"That's as good a place as any," Julian decided, and ran out the door, Oscar promptly following.

Derek remained still, waiting for them to go.

He felt bad about lying.

But he had to.

Julian did not believe in good. Oscar was too clouded by love.

And only Derek knew the true depths of this demon.

Madelina had taken herself to a place of suicide to prevent further death. To a steep hill.

That was where Derek knew April would be.

And, as he turned his body and placed his feet on the cold floor, he knew it would take the final energy he had left to get to her.

He took the clothes hidden beneath the bed and put them on. Once he had tied his laces, he made his way to the door, and checked that the coast was clear.

36

Cleeve Hill. The highest point of any hill in the Cotswolds. In the heart of Gloucestershire, next to Cheltenham, April's beloved home town.

The higher points meant steeper drops – and April had found the perfect height, with the perfect fatal fall.

It would be great.

The view before her brought back a sense of nostalgia. Memories of being a little girl, holding her daddy's hand as he guided her up here. Back in the years before he died. Before she was homeless.

She remembered one Christmas Eve in particular. She had been restless, eagerly anticipating the morning that was to follow. Santa Claus was coming and, although she didn't believe in him, she couldn't quell her excitement. So much so, she could not sit still. So her dad had brought her up here for a walk, a walk that lasted all afternoon, so she could expend that energy. It was one of the happiest times she'd had. Probably the happiest memory she had before the age of fourteen. When it all went so terribly wrong.

That memory made this location all the more ideal.

A perfect circle. A happy place to end a mostly happy life.

Oscar would miss her. Would he cope?

Surely, he must.

He had coped fine before she arrived.

Actually, that was a lie. He'd been a loser, spending his days working a dead-end job, playing on his Xbox all night, and jacking off in his room.

She gently snorted a reminiscent smile to her face.

You never realise the impact your mere presence or involvement in another's life has until you are about to take that presence away.

But did she have a choice?

It was not the demon inside of her telling her to end this. It was the human.

Just as it was the human inside of her that ensured she did not kill Julian. That she did not put enough benzodiazepines into Oscar's soup to be fatal. The human that had stopped her from killing more than the mere number of children she has killed so far.

But the children she had killed... that she had torn apart, unable to do anything but watch....

Her fingers were warily slipping. Her control over this part of her was being relinquished, and she could feel her thoughts losing any resemblance of sense.

What would happen to her once it had grown stronger?

What would happen once it had been born?

No.

She loved Oscar. She loved him more than life.

But that was why she had to do this.

That was why she had to save him.

He'd stop her. If he was here, he'd insist there was another way. He'd do anything to pull her back, to rip her away from the lethal drop.

She didn't even know what this thing inside of her was.

Was it a human baby?

A demon?

Some bizarre, deadly concoction of the two?

She rubbed her hands over her belly. She could feel it kick. Reacting to her touch. Responding with aggression.

She bowed her head. Allowed a rogue tear to drift into the wind.

She would not let herself cry. She would not let herself feel regret, remorse, or hesitance over what she was about to do.

So why hadn't she done it yet?

She stepped forward, the sight beneath her making her knees buckle and her stomach lurch. Such a drop, inches from her toes, staring back at her. Giving her the sense of imminent dread.

Her arms lifted out to the side like she was mounted to an invisible cross. She closed her eyes and spread her fingers, to allow the breeze to brush between them, to comb the air with its refreshing moisture.

It was a perfect day.

Not too cold, not too warm. A slight draught that did nothing to push her backward or forward.

It was the kind of day she and Oscar would enjoy spending together, climbing a hill like Cleeve Hill, revisiting through the memories that both of them shared. Some good. Some bad. And some with no emotional attachment whatsoever.

She dropped her head, her chin pressing against her chest.

She opened her eyes with a narrow slit.

The drop before her no longer made her knees buckle.

No longer made her queasy.

No longer frightened her.

It was the sight of inevitability. The sight of no going back. The sight of absolutely no choice but this one.

Choice.

It was a word people rarely acquired the meaning of in their life.

She was making a choice, but it wasn't hers.

It had never been hers.

She readied herself.

It was time.

37

SEEING THAT DEREK WAS STRUGGLING AND HOBBLING ON HIS walking stick, the taxi driver stepped out of the car and helped him to the backseat. He held the car door open and placed a helpful hand on Derek's back, waiting patiently as Derek feebly levered himself down using the headrest of the seat in front of him.

As Derek sat he readjusted himself and grabbed the seatbelt. Nodding at the taxi driver that he was ready, the taxi driver took to his seat as Derek put his biceps into work, pulling the seat belt across his front and pushing it into its slot.

"You okay?" the taxi driver asked.

"Fine," Derek responded.

"Where to?"

Derek thought. He knew the type of location he was going to, but his mind was already weakly racing across what words he could possibly say that would be more successful than with Madelina, and he hadn't yet thought which hill to go to.

"Where is the nearest, steepest hill?" Derek asked.

The driver thought for a moment.

"Cleeve Hill, I guess?" he offered with a quizzical look, as if it was the best answer he could give.

"Good," Derek confirmed, happy with the choice. "Then I would like to go there."

"Right you are."

The taxi driver turned, put his seatbelt on, rotated the key in the ignition, and pulled onto the road.

"Please, may we be hasty?" Derek asked. "My needs are desperate, and I'd appreciate some valour in your speed."

"'Scuse me?"

"Erm – please, can we be quick?"

Derek had always had a way with words that often left other people wondering what he meant.

"Right you are." The driver pulled into the fast lane.

Derek leant his head back, using the headrest to soften the blow.

How was it he felt so bad? That everything was such a task? That every action took the energy that would have previously been expended in a 5K run?

He had come to terms with death a while ago. The illness had only confirmed that the inevitable drew closer, and he was prepared.

The only thing he was not prepared for was leaving anything unfinished.

Madelina. April. Julian.

These were all unfinished.

He had to get there. He had to.

He allowed his head to loll, dropping onto his shoulder, and his mind drifted into an absent sleep. His mind filled with emptiness, allowing him a precious passage of time where imminent death or demonic spawn were not so prevalent in his thoughts.

He was awoken to the driver pushing him on the shoulder.

"We're here."

Derek looked out the window. There was a narrow road that went up the hill.

"Please, can you take me as far up the hill as you can?"

The driver looked at the path, then back to Derek, his eyebrows raised.

"Please. It is of the utmost importance."

The taxi driver reluctantly shrugged and did as he was instructed. Derek watched as the hills went by, peering into the distance, trying to see if he could spot a lonely woman on the verge of suicide.

What if he was too late?

What if all he'd see was a mangled corpse at the bottom of a steep drop?

"This is as far as I can go," the driver announced after a few minutes.

"Thank you ever so much." Derek scrambled through his pocket for a few wayward coins, and placed them in the driver's rough hand. "Keep the change."

"Cheers, mate."

Derek pushed the door open and moved across the stony ground, wincing at the bumps in the base of his shoe.

"You sure you're going to be all right?" the driver inquired. "You really don't look in the best state to be wandering around hills."

"I'll be fine."

"Are you sure, mate, 'cause–"

"I said I'll be fine!" Derek snapped, tiredness getting the better of him.

"Right you are!" the driver snapped back. He drove the car away at an excessive speed for a one-way country lane.

Derek paused, waiting for the energy to refill his legs. He peered across the horizon, over all the bumpy hills, seeking out a figure that would give him a direction.

He was going to have to use the final breaths he had. The

final stiffness of his muscles, the final twisting of his aching bones. He was going to have to force a surge of energy into his fading body, and will himself to battle on.

For everything he had faced, finding that required energy without collapsing was going to be the biggest battle he had yet.

Finally, his strained vision picked out something on the next hill over. An excessively steep drop, with a woman tipping gently over it. She looked ready. Like she was seconds from ending her life.

Derek had no time to waste.

He moved his walking stick forward and began his most trying journey yet.

38

OSCAR CHARGED OUT OF JULIAN'S CAR TOWARD THE PHARMACY, but all he found was a locked door and the dark interior of a shop shut for the day. He shook the door, battling against it, his frustration reaching the surface.

"Damn it!" he cursed.

Julian appeared behind him.

"Fuck!" Oscar continued to vent. "Where else is there? Erm, there is the coffee shop we used to go to, we could look there? Maybe we could go–"

"Oscar," Julian interrupted. "If she doesn't want to be found, chances are she won't go there."

"But Derek said–"

"Derek is delusional. He's ill. He doesn't really know what he's saying."

Oscar paused, trying to think of another solution. He didn't stay still for long before he was racing back to the car.

"Well, we've still got to try!" he insisted.

"Oscar," Julian said once more, forcing Oscar to turn around and throw his arms into the air.

"What?"

"We have to think about something."

"What? Right now?"

"Yes." Julian stepped forward, doing all he could to keep an air of calmness. "What are we going to do when we find her? *If* we find her?"

"What do you mean?"

"As in, what's our plan?"

Oscar shrugged.

"Do we need one?"

"Just an idea. What are we going to do?"

"We are going to save her."

"Save her?"

"At least try."

"What if she can't be saved?"

"You heard what Derek said–"

Julian rolled his eyes and let out a big, angry sigh.

"Stop quoting Derek to me!" Julian grudgingly insisted. "He was a great man, but now…"

"Well I believe him. I have to. Because I know damn well that if anyone tries to do anything but save her, they will do it over my dead body."

Oscar turned and resumed marching toward the car.

"Maybe that's why you should leave me to find her alone," Julian suggested.

"Are you kidding me?"

"After all, I've known her a lot longer than you. I know her better. I could get through to her more."

"Fuck you, Julian. Fuck off with your pathetic little ego! I've had enough of your cynical, constantly whiny attitude, especially not *right* now – especially with what is at stake!"

Oscar couldn't help it. His lip quivered. Prompting tears to edge out of his eyes.

"If Derek was able to think, if he knew what he was doing, he'd have sent us on this wild good chase for a reason," Julian said. "He's quite clearly sent us to the wrong location. Why do you think he'd have done that?"

"I don't know, Julian!"

"I would imagine because he knows we can't save her. That he knows he's full of shit."

"I thought you said he didn't know what he was doing?"

Oscar shook his head with uncompromising confidence, a sneer in his upturned lip refusing to accept anything but his own truth.

"I think *you* are the one full of shit, Julian. You're not right all the time. And if you think you are going to stop me from looking, however hopeless it may be, then you can go to hell. Because I will smash that car's windows down and drive it away myself if you are going to refuse."

Julian nodded. He walked to the driver's seat and got in, Oscar sitting beside him.

"Where to?" Julian asked.

"The coffee shop we used to go to. The little one with the curtains in the windows."

"Okay."

Julian drove, and as he did, they maintained a tense silence.

Oscar's fingers clawed into the side of his seat. He couldn't think. He couldn't do anything until he knew she was safe. By whatever means necessary, he had to know April and his daughter were safe.

A few minutes later, Julian pulled into a vacant space opposite the coffee shop.

It was closed. Pitch black. Empty.

Another wrong answer.

Oscar's head dropped.

"Do you believe me now?" Julian asked.

"Wetherspoons."

"What?"

"The Wetherspoons toilets where she found she was pregnant. Try there next."

"Oscar, she isn't going to be–"

"Try there!"

Julian sighed and pulled away.

Oscar knew it was hopeless.

He knew she wouldn't be there.

But he didn't know what else to do.

39

His legs were seizing. Pain soaring through his throbbing muscles until they felt like they were going to fall to shreds. His bones wobbled as if the earth was shaking, but it was not; it was the feebleness of the bones that had already begun to decay. His body shook with a hot fever, quivering harsher than the worst flu he'd ever suffered.

But what hurt him most was the sight before him.

A lonely woman. Lost. With no other choice.

As Derek finally stepped upon the grassy verge leading to April's tormented body, his knees gave way and he fell onto his front.

But he did not pass out. He did not allow himself. He had to keep her talking, keep doing something, whatever he could to ensure she did not throw herself off that steep drop.

Her head turned to the side. Her body remained stiffly facing the edge of the hill, her face turned half over her shoulder.

She was not surprised.

"April..." Derek tried, his hoarse voice breaking under the

strain. It was rough like sandpaper, gristly in his sore throat. "April… stop…"

"What are you doing here?" her quiet, sombre voice replied as her face turned back to her fate.

Derek went to speak.

Why was he there?

He had expended such energy on the steep slope to reach her, his diminishing thoughts hadn't grasped any reason or words that he could use to justify her changing her decision.

He pushed himself to his knees, where he remained. He hoped she thought this was him begging. In truth, the edges of his vision were turning to black blurs, and he was unable to find the ability to stand.

"You can't do this," he said in the most compelling voice he had possible.

"You shouldn't be here."

Her body shifted her weight slightly forward, edging ever nearer to death.

"You don't think that," Derek claimed. "Or you would have done it already."

Fool!

He scolded himself for his poor lexical choice. Tempting her to complete her task was not what he intended to do.

Her foot stepped forward so that only her heel remained on solid ground. It knocked a few stones, sending them collapsing into the abyss.

"I once knew a girl. A sweet Portuguese woman, about the same age as you, who suffered the same trials."

April's head shook with marginal movement.

"I did," Derek persisted. "She was a nurse. She lived in Edinburgh. And by God, she was an infectious soul. A sparkling personality, enriching everyone she knew. Just like you."

"I've not been feeling very infectious lately," she replied, her voice remaining in a dull monotone. It was as if she had ripped all emotion out of her speech.

"I've noticed," Derek admitted. He allowed himself a few minutes to think, a few minutes to conjure the solutions that never clearly presented themselves.

"I see Oscar didn't come. Or Julian."

"They wanted to, April. Oh, they wanted to. But I sent them the other way."

"Why?"

"Because they aren't like me, you see. They don't believe that good can conquer the world. They don't believe that good can save you."

She shook her head, wiping her eyes on her sleeve.

"And *you* do?"

"Oh God, yes. Absolutely. I have always believed it. I wouldn't be good at what I do if I didn't."

A sharp pang fired through Derek's chest. A tingling shot up and down his left arm. His elbows gave way and he collapsed onto his chest.

Still, he remained resolute.

Still, he watched her.

"I can hear your heart," she told him. "It's fading. Getting quieter. Slower."

"I'm dying, April. I've known it for a while. The last few weeks, I've just been sitting in my bed, waiting for it."

She vaguely nodded. "I know what that's like."

"There's a difference. You have a choice."

"No, I don't!" she screamed, the first sign of anger coming from her.

This was good.

Derek could use this.

"This thing is inside of me!"

"No, your daughter is inside of you."

"No, it's not!"

"The demon is attached to your daughter, April. Your demon is not your daughter, it is attached, I promise, it is. We can do something about this."

"How?"

"Just like we've done with every other demon that's attached itself to a poor soul. We have... We've..."

He coughed.

"We've..."

He coughed again.

"We've... w..."

A splatter of blood dripped from his mouth, staining the moonlit grass beneath him. The flakes of green had turned to flakes of dark brown; dead plantation providing a rough bed for his chest.

"Please, April... I'm dy–... I'm..."

April turned her head to her shoulder once more.

Something ran down her thigh. Something wet.

She looked down.

It trickled down her leg.

Her water had broken. She was in labour.

She looked at the drop. This was it.

"Please, April..."

"Don't try to save me."

"We can help... You can be saved..."

She closed her eyes.

Spread her arms like wings.

Tipped forward.

"Goodbye, Derek."

40

"Oscar loves you," Derek spluttered between mouthfuls of blood.

April halted. She could feel the pain in his chest. It reached out to her. It penetrated her heart until she felt it all.

She felt everything. Saw everything. Knew the longing of Derek.

Such was her ability to feel the pain of the dead. Ever since Julian had first taught her what her powers as a conduit meant, she had always been able to channel the deceased, in a way that–

Wait...

She leant back. Her arms dropped to the side.

Her thoughts repeated on her.

She was able to channel Derek's thoughts.

But I can only channel the thoughts of the deceased.

"Derek?" she asked.

No reply.

She turned to look at him.

She could feel his desperation to save her. His true, persistent belief in the good in her. His hope that his words could provide the encouragement she needed to survive.

She was a vessel for the non-living. Which meant…

She bowed her head. Closed her eyes. Denied it. However counterproductive it was, her thoughts denied it.

Derek laid on his front. Eyes closed. Chest still. Breath non-existent.

But she could feel him. Just as she had done with that old man who killed the girl for the very first time four years ago, she felt the dead close by.

Only this time, the feelings were different. They weren't of rage and anger.

They were of hope.

Optimism.

Positivity.

Derek sunk through her, filling her mind, filling her blood, pushing into her thoughts.

This was her gift. She could feel the emotions of those she channelled, could feel their lives.

She was in Derek's mind, looking through his eyes. In his sick bed. Alone.

She had a cup of tea in her hands.

She felt so weak. So weary. So empty of energy and life and–

Oscar.

He smiled back at Derek. Smiled back at her.

By his bedside. In the midst of simple conversation.

"But this child wasn't planned," she heard Derek's voice say through her lips. "How are you going to cope?"

Oscar's eyes twinkled with excitement as they looked back at her.

"With great energy and enthusiasm, my friend," Oscar asserted. "When I'm with April, it's like – I'm not just a better person, but I am the truest person I am. Like, everything changes."

She felt Derek smile. Felt his happiness. His appreciation of Oscar's feelings.

A tear fell down her cheek.

She fell to her knees.

She watched the memory. Felt the genuine love exuding from Oscar. Felt Derek's soul as it reached out to Oscar and his kind words, as Oscar's face melted into ecstasy at the thought.

"The world just sinks away, and it's me and her. Us against the world. And now it's going to be us three. And, I – I can't wait."

"What if the baby–"

"I don't care. I know what you're about to say, and whatever the baby brings, I will do whatever to protect that child, and to protect April."

Oscar's eyes focussed on Derek's.

After everything that had happened. Her absence from their conscious lives. Her troubles, her anger, her hostility.

After everything that had happened, he still spoke so clearly and so resolutely.

"She has changed my life. And I can never repay that."

She collapsed to the floor.

Derek's hope and enthusiasm fell out of her like water through fingers. He left.

She was alone again in her body.

Next to Derek's.

More alone than she had ever been.

She collapsed into a weeping mess.

This child could be evil.

But Oscar would do anything.

Oscar.

That boy. That strange, brilliant boy.

She cried uncontrollable tears, weeping, pushing them out of her eyes until there was nothing left to cry.

She turned to Derek. His face empty. His hollow eyes now open.

Her legs were covered in fluid.

This baby, whatever it was, was on its way.

She took her mobile out of her pocket and dialled 999.

"Hello, I'm at the top of Cleeve Hill," she said. "I've just gone into labour."

41

WHAT ON EARTH IS GOING TO COME OUT OF HER?

Since receiving the call from the hospital on his and Julian's drive away from the coffee shop, those were the words occupying Oscar's mind, spinning around like a bad animation on a PowerPoint presentation.

She was already in delivery. Whatever it was coming out of her, it was eager to arrive.

He burst through the hospital doors, charged to reception and, with a voice full of frantic anticipatory trepidation, he said to the receptionist, "Where is the maternity ward? My girlfriend's gone into labour."

"Down the corridor, up the stairs to the third floor, and to your right."

He walked as fast as he could without running, having to quickly adjust his path to avoid a few nurses. He directed himself to the stairs, and heard nothing put the patter of his feet quickly tapping against the steps.

Julian wasn't with him – something he was secretly glad of. This wasn't a time for Julian's cynical interference.

Although, the reason for Julian's absence wasn't so cele-bratory.

Julian received a call at almost precisely the time he had, from a separate department in the hospital, to be informed that Derek had been taken to the intensive care ward, and they were currently battling for his life.

Oscar hoped Derek survived.

It was a shame that such an occasion as a child's birth had to coincide with such a solemn turn of events.

Then again, the past few months had all been a solemn turn of events. And there was never an opportune moment to face death.

His shoulder barged into the door of the third floor and he gave up the hasty walk for a spirited run, aiming straight for the reception desk.

"Hi, my girlfriend's in labour."

"What's her name?"

"April Cristine."

The nurse looked at a sheet in front of her. Oscar wished she would hurry up.

"What's your name?"

"Oscar."

"Okay, Oscar, come with me."

The nurse led Oscar down the corridor, so slowly he kept knocking into her. It was as if nothing was happening. He kept thinking – *does this woman not know my child is being born?*

After a small walk that felt uncomfortably long, the nurse reached a curtain and pulled it aside.

"We have the father here," the nurse said.

"Send him in."

The nurse turned to Oscar.

"Here you are."

Oscar brushed the curtain aside and stood inside.

April was on the bed in a sterile hospital gown, her eyelids drooping and her head lolling to the side. A doctor sat between her open legs, the sight of a head in his hands. A nurse was by April's side, but as soon as this nurse saw Oscar, she moved aside so that Oscar could take her place.

He took April's sweaty hand firmly in his and brushed her hair out of her face.

"It's okay," he told her. "I'm here now."

Her fingers loosely flexed, then remained limp.

"How's she doing?" Oscar asked the doctor.

"Okay, but she's been in and out of consciousness. We've lost a lot of blood, but we're on the home stretch now."

Oscar turned back to April. Looked at her face. Her absent, pale face, her scabbed laps, her perspiring brow. She looked a state, to everyone else but him – to Oscar, this was the woman he loved.

"Right, April, you need to push," the doctor demanded. "I need you to stay with us, and push."

April groaned, her head turning to the side, her eyes remaining closed.

"Come on, April, I know you can do this."

Oscar kissed her forehead.

Then the fear returned.

What on earth is going to come out of her?

He pictured a demonic child. Horns. Flailing limbs. Snake tail for legs. Fire from its throat.

But as the doctor kept reminding April to push, he gave no indication of shock or horror by a strange appearance of the baby.

Oscar stayed by her side, holding her hand, whispering in her ear. She wasn't all there. Her eyes fluttered every now and then, but he knew she could hear him. He knew he had to keep talking to her, to keep her alive.

The piercing sound of a baby's wail filled the vicinity.

Oscar stared at the doctor, waiting for a reaction. A retort such as, "Oh dear God," or, "What the hell is that?"

The doctor did no such thing.

Instead, he smiled. Cut the umbilical cord and gave the child to the nurse, who checked her breath, clearing a small strip of fluid from her nose. She wrapped the baby in a towel, then turned to Oscar.

"Would you like to hold her?" she asked.

Oscar shook. He was nervous. He had a fluttering excitement in his belly, like he had on his first date with April.

Why am I so nervous?

He stepped forward, yet to see the baby's true form. He reached his arms out, slowly taking the baby, supporting her head, and brought her to his chest.

The baby stopped crying.

She looked up at Oscar with a perplexed look, as if to say, "I've never seen you before."

She was beautiful.

Her arms and legs wriggled like a tiny human. Her fingers reached out and clamped around one of his. Her eyes were big and green, staring up at his.

There were no tentacles.

No snake tails.

No horns.

She was an innocent, gorgeous little girl.

And Oscar could not have been filled with more love and adoration for the tiny person he cradled.

Being transfixed by her, his senses became suddenly aware of a commotion. The doctor was at April's side, shouting nonsensical instructions at the nurse that Oscar couldn't understand.

April's eyes weren't fluttering. Her fingers weren't lifting. Her face was blank.

"Is she okay?" Oscar asked.

He was ignored.

"Doctor, please, is she going to be okay?"

"Yes, but we still need to see to her – give us some space."

As a few more nurses came to the doctor's side, the maternity nurse who had handed Oscar his baby girl guided him away.

"Come on, let's get her cleaned up," she said.

"Is April going to be okay?" Oscar persisted, clutching onto his daughter, but desperately worried about her mother.

"Yes, but she has had a lot of difficulties, and we still have some work to do. We agreed before the birth that we would give her some Vitamin K to prevent haemorrhagic disease. Do you remember?"

"Erm, yeah, I guess," he answered, his mind barely registering what she was saying. But he let her guide him into another room, just hoping that April would be okay.

42

JULIAN'S LEGS CARRIED HIM BACK AND FORTH, FROM ONE SIDE OF the empty waiting room to the other. He wished he could halt his incessant pacing, but his legs wouldn't allow it.

The waiting room was decorated with blue paint and pictures of families. He understood why they had chosen such a calming colour, but the families he could not understand. This was the waiting room for intensive care, the place where families are most likely to be destroyed. Why would you want to see a happy family whilst yours is being ripped away?

He ran through every interaction he'd ever had with Derek. Every argument, every nasty word, every act of defiance. Every belittlement, every disagreement, every protest.

Suddenly, he felt like he'd been excessively cruel to his mentor. Made Derek feel guilty about Julian having to take care of him, despite Julian not actually being that bothered.

He knew his guilt was surfacing because he faced the possibility of losing him. That there were plenty of good memories too. It was just that, in that moment, his mind would not let him see them.

The door opened slowly and a doctor entered.

Julian stopped pacing. Stuck rigidly to the floor. Staring wide-eyed. The stillest he had been since he'd entered that room

"Julian?" the doctor asked.

"Yes," Julian confirmed. "How is he? Is he okay?"

The doctor's head bowed momentarily as he gathered his thoughts.

Julian knew what that meant.

He knew *exactly* what that meant.

"We did everything we could," the doctor said. "The cancer had spread too far. It had reached the lining of his heart – which made it almost impossible for us to start it again."

"Is he–"

Julian couldn't say it.

He couldn't say the word.

But he didn't have to.

The doctor faintly nodded.

"He lived longer than we expected," the doctor assured. "That last climb up the hill he did – it was one too many."

Julian didn't know what to say. His eyes remained focussed on the doctor.

"I'm sorry for your loss," the doctor said, and turned to go.

"Can I see him?" Julian asked.

The doctor hesitated.

"Yes," he finally answered. "The coroner is on his way, but you may have a few minutes first. Follow me."

Julian followed the doctor toward the operating theatre. Outside of it, Julian saw several surgeons, doctors, and nurses, all with solemn faces. They looked to Julian, understanding who he was, and all gave him an instinctive sympathetic smile.

He wished they hadn't.

They'd be back to work that next morning.

Julian wouldn't.

Not after this.

The doctor opened the door and allowed Julian to walk in. The doctor remained at the entrance as Julian slowly made his way toward a bed with a motionless body laid upon it. Numerous lights were fixed overhead, and surgical equipment remained on trays, still yet to be cleaned.

Julian reached Derek's side.

Derek's eyes were closed. Which Julian was grateful for.

A sharp pang cursed his chest, accompanied by the thought that he'd let him down. That he'd not listened to him. That maybe if he'd have paid attention to Derek's final lesson, things would be different.

Unsure whether he was thinking this out of grief or honesty, he willed the thoughts from his mind.

He took hold of Derek's hand. It was already stiff. Already cold.

He thought of what to say.

What his final words could be.

To the mentor he'd always wished for. The father figure he'd never before been granted.

To the man who taught him everything.

To the man who had taken more of Julian's shit than anybody else.

To the man who had never stopped trying. No matter how much Julian pushed, how much he tried it on, kept his own stubborn opinion, everyone else left. Hated him for his pessimistic outbursts.

Derek never left.

Never.

He remained. Loyal as a man could wish for.

What do you say to someone like that? What final words do you give them?

Deciding that he could never articulate the true lamentations of his affection, he settled for two very simple words.

"Thank you."

43

A GRAVEYARD.

Weeks and weeks of tracking Derek, which had turned into months, and turned into years, and that was where he found him.

Martin wished it wasn't so.

He stood over the headstone of his former mentor. The closest thing to a friend he'd ever had.

Truth was, he hadn't even found Derek. Martin was still listed as Derek's emergency contact. *They* had found *him*.

And now, with no face to look at, no skin to touch, he wondered what he was supposed to feel.

Anger? Not at Derek, but at his own stupidity. His own ridiculous, stubborn nature that meant Derek's attempts to reconcile had fallen on deaf ears.

Remorse? That his final words to Derek had been too harsh?

Regret?

No.

It surprised him, but he felt numb. It was as he was

expecting it. Like this was how he imagined his next interaction with Derek would be.

He turned and walked away. He wasn't one for sentimentality. He'd seen what he'd needed to see, now it was time to go.

As he made his way down a gravel path, he could see another man walking toward Derek's gravestone. He paused, and watched him.

The man looked sad, yet strong. Late twenties. Hands over his face.

Was this one of Derek's friends?

Had Derek moved on and found other people to help?

Had Derek even remembered Martin?

Ridiculous, really. A selfish thought. What, did he expect Derek to mope around for ten years, wishing Martin had ended the feud Martin had caused? Perhaps he just felt bitter that he'd been living alone all this time, and Derek had surrounded himself with people.

Derek always was more of a people person than he was.

The man's hands dropped. His eyes were red, wet with tears. His head slowly turned, and he looked at Martin.

Their eyes met, and held each other's gaze. No expressions, no hostility, no smiles – just watching each other across the crowded graves. Ignoring the bustle of the wind.

Martin wondered who this was.

A man trained by Derek, maybe. A man with a deep caring for him.

Did Derek rescue this man from a life of delinquency and potential crime, just like he had when Martin was young?

He tried to talk to the man. To open his mouth, give a message of condolence, to state that he was sad, regretful, morose. But he wasn't. He was numb. And he couldn't come out and say this.

The only positive Martin could find was that the demon's

taunts were incorrect. The demon that had defeated him had claimed that the devil was preparing vengeance on Derek. That someone was going to be pregnant with demon spawn. That this would heap pain over Derek's weakening temperament.

But with Derek dead, there would be no point making someone close to him pregnant now. Vengeance against Derek would be pointless if Derek wasn't there to suffer through it.

So at least Martin knew that the demon was wrong.

Which meant he had no reason to stay. He needn't warn this man of anything.

He gave a gentle but definite nod to this man, who gave one in return.

Martin thought about what his next step was. Maybe he could reinvent himself. Find a life away from the demonic. Get married. Get a job. Fall in love.

But, somehow, he knew that the demonic would always find him.

Bury himself underground, then. Become a recluse. Be that crazy man who lives alone in a house that children run past. Maybe he could even grow a beard.

Finally ceasing eye contact, he stepped forward, directing his feet out of the graveyard and away from the life he left behind.

He'd tried to track Derek down because he needed to warn him.

But Derek was dead now.

Which meant, just as he expected the demon was full of lies.

There was no demon baby. No vengeful demons. No warnings he needed to give.

There was nothing for him there. There never was. He was a nomad without a purpose. A drifter without a home. A man without a soul in the world to care.

He reached the car park, got into his car, and drove away, watching the graveyard grow smaller in his rear-view mirror, thinking of nothing but regrets.

ONE MONTH LATER

44

HAYLEY'S EYES REMAINED SOUNDLY CLOSED. HER DELICATE SKIN wrapped up, and the pram shielding her face from the sun. This was the quietest she'd been all day, and Oscar was grateful for the moment's peace as she slept.

Though, as tired as he was, he ended up missing the moments when she was awake.

It was tough doing this alone.

"Do you ever think," Oscar suggested, "that we could ever have a normal life?"

Julian, sitting on the bench beside him, smiled in a playfully dismissive manner.

"Us? Normal?" Julian joked. "We can't do normal anymore. We've seen too much."

"Yeah. Don't disagree with you."

Julian peered at the sleeping child. The sweet girl moving in her sleep. So cute. So tiny.

"So she didn't end up with tentacles then?" Julian mused.

"No," Oscar answered, smiling at Julian's incredulous humour. "She turned out to be a beautiful, wonderful baby girl.

Whatever evil forces surrounded Hayley, I've seen no evidence of them."

Julian nodded, still watching the child.

"I'm glad," he said honestly. "Really, I am. I know I was a bit of a dick about it, but, honestly – you and April, you're meant for each other."

"Wow. Have you hit your head or something?"

"Don't push it. I've said something nice to you; that's mine done for another year."

Oscar chuckled. Then his face fell and his smile dropped.

He missed April.

"Have you seen her lately?" Julian asked, knowing exactly what the change in Oscar's face had indicated.

"Yeah, I took Hayley to see her yesterday."

"Any word?"

Oscar stuck out his bottom lip and aimlessly shook his head.

"I'm sure it's just a matter of time," Julian reassured Oscar.

"Yeah. I hope."

"She's strong. She'll fight."

"I don't know. Even the doctors don't know why she's still not waking up. She's fine, they just… can't figure it out."

"Here's a secret, and it's something I've learnt from a few years in our business – but the doctors don't always know everything."

"Yeah… that's what I'm worried about. What if it's not something of this world? If the thing that was supposed to have the baby now has her?"

Julian struggled for an answer. And Oscar knew why.

Twice now, they had denied that paranormal attacks on them were happening – Anna haunting Julian last year, and April's bizarre pregnancy.

It seemed like something was stepping up its attacks. Was targeting them.

And Oscar didn't blame them.

The work that the Sensitives had done against hell, against demons, had been brilliant so far. In truth, they had barely scraped the surface, but they had announced their presence as people to be reckoned with.

They couldn't have a few successes without expecting a backlash.

"What's next?" Oscar asked.

"What do you mean?"

"I mean, you've been targeted. Derek's been targeted. April's been targeted. That just leaves me."

"They won't go after you."

"Why not?"

"You're too strong. Too good. And they won't take a battle they don't think they can win."

Oscar looked at Julian, spiritedly bemused.

"That's two nice things now," he pointed out.

"Yeah, I know. I'm starting to feel sick."

They chuckled.

Hayley murmured, so Oscar placed his palm on her forehead and she sank back into her sleep.

"I know it was inevitable. I'm just worried about who it is that's coming after us. *What* it is. I mean, what's going to–"

"Oscar, Oscar," Julian interrupted, "just enjoy your successes. April is still alive. Your baby is healthy. You are here."

"Since when were you one to see the good in things?"

Julian smiled. "It was a lesson I had to learn."

For a few minutes, they allowed a comfortable silence to settle between them. The sun beamed against their skin, forcing Julian to remove his jacket. They watched people go by, minding their own business, dealing with their own problems.

Thinking they were safe.

Just as Oscar thought he was. Just as Julian thought he was.

They had fended off the attacks that had come at them enough times to feel a sense of resilience.

Safe. For now.

Just as they assumed Hayley was too.

Oscar's baby had been born. She was a perfect representation of hope. The product of positive thinking. A wonderful child who cried and smiled like any other.

To Oscar, she was perfect. He stared down at her with no worries in his mind as to what she could be – they had all been quelled, and his mind was at ease.

A head. Two arms. Two legs. A round belly. A mouth that could scream and laugh. Normal as normal could be.

But she wasn't normal.

There was a reason this child's mother lay inexplicably comatose.

There was a reason the child gave the illusion of being perfect.

There was a reason the child had been born.

And her loving father, cooing down at her, was blissfully unaware of any of it.

DEMON'S DAUGHTER

RICK WOOD

JOIN RICK WOOD'S READER'S GROUP FOR YOUR FREE BOOKS

Join at **www.rickwoodwriter.com/sign-up**

Printed in Great Britain
by Amazon

39353913R00148